PRETTY EVIL

A DARK MAFIA ROMANCE

THE DARK LORDS

STELLA ANDREWS

NEWSLETTER

Sign up to my newsletter and download a free eBook.

stellaandrews.com

THE DARK LORDS

PRETTY EVIL

When the cage door opens, freedom is a difficult temptation to ignore.
Serena Vieri
Mafia princess, protected her entire life for a very good reason.

There is a target on her back.

Her family believed she was better off not knowing but with knowledge comes a certain kind of power that she could sure use right now.
On her way to Australia to see her mom, her bodyguard was detained leaving her open to attack.
The attack came in the form of whispered words of adventure.
A deep husky voice promised her the flight of her life.
He slid over her soul like a serpent about to strike and trapped her in a web of intrigue and desire.
He thought he had the upper hand.

He was wrong.

Serena Vieri learned her lessons well and he is about to discover that some journeys require you to hold on tight if you want to arrive at your destination in one piece.

A dark mafia romance that will hold you prisoner until the end.

Book three of The Dark Lords.
Book one is **Pure Evil**
Book Two is **A Shade of Evil**

PROLOGUE

SERENA

*M*y heart is heavy, and the tears burn as the car takes me away from the only people I love and trust with all my heart. As send offs go, this one is bittersweet because now my brothers have introduced two other females into our tight circle, I am interested in getting to know them.

I almost pity them and wonder if they understand what they have let themselves in for.

It's not easy being a Vieri and especially not a woman. I'm just surprised I was allowed to go and visit the one who got away.

Mom lives in Australia, and you couldn't get much further than that, but she obviously decided it was her best shot at happiness when she divorced my father.

I miss her and I'm desperate to reconnect with her. It's just a shame I must travel halfway across the world to do it.

As I watch the familiar scenery passing, I gaze out of the window and wonder if I will be as happy as my brothers obviously are because I never have much luck meeting guys. When your brothers head up the local mafia, there really aren't that many takers.

Then there's me. I am made of the same stuff and I'm not the innocent young woman many guys like to have by their side. I'm a challenge. I realize that and I won't ever be anything else.

The three cars in our cavalcade must be an interesting sight as we speed on our way to the airport. My grandfather wanted me to take a private plane, but I insisted on traveling in a commercial one. I want to be among normal people for once. To live their life and merge into the shadows. I don't want to be Serena Vieri, the mafia princess. I want to be Serena Vieri, a daughter visiting her mom.

I'm dressed in black leggings and a black hoody, my hair hiding under a black baseball cap. I'm wearing sneakers and carrying a black leather holdall, my luggage in the car behind. I am invisible. At least I certainly hope so and the only stipulation my grandfather insisted on was that Connor came with me.

He sits in the car in front, on red alert and watching out for danger, and my heart sinks. When will I ever be free of this shit? Trust me to travel with a bodyguard. An assassin who doesn't require a weapon to protect me when his hands are more than adequate for the job.

I'm guessing he's not that happy about it either, and I almost feel sorry for him. Almost. The trouble is, I'm too busy feeling sorry for myself.

WE REACH the airport in no time at all and as the cars pull to a stop, the doors open, and the occupants spill out like an oil slick. Black suits, black shades, and black souls form a tight guard of honor as my cases are loaded onto a trolley. I must wait until the door is opened and as I step outside, the black shades covering my own eyes cause passers-by to stare. They will wonder if I'm a celebrity. That can be the only explanation because the mafia isn't something ordinary people think a lot about.

I follow Connor into the terminal, toward the first-class

check in and as I wait, I note the curious glances thrown my way from a nearby line. As always, the guards crowd around me and I sigh inside. Not long now and I will be free. For the next three weeks, anyway.

We check in and the agent stares at me with interest as she hands me the boarding card with a polite smile.

"The first-class lounge is through security and to your right, up the escalator and toward the back, near Starbucks."

"Thanks." I smile and Connor takes the boarding passes and says to the nearest guard, "Keep eyes on us through security. Report any problems in the usual way."

They nod and as we walk toward the fast-track security point, it's as if I leave behind the burden that sits heavily on my shoulders.

Soon I will be free. Nothing can touch me when I reach my destination and with a happy heart I leave all my troubles behind and head into security and I don't look back.

ALEXEI

She enters the lounge as if she doesn't belong here. I observe from my table as I eat a fine lunch for one, unusually alone.

The man with her is obviously paid protection, judging from the way his eyes scan the room and he appears on edge.

I stare with interest at the girl. A slight figure dressed head to toe in black, with no designers present in her wardrobe. If I saw her on the street, I wouldn't look twice, but there is something about this scene that interests me.

I carry on eating and the guard ushers her into a booth before sitting opposite and scanning the area.

A waitress stops and hands them a menu each and as she

studies it, the man with her glares around him with an air of menace that warns anyone from approaching.

The fact I'm here at all is an irritant I'm still dealing with. Usually, I travel on my private jet, but a technical issue at the last minute had me boarding a commercial flight instead.

I have no time to wait for an engineer because business comes before my comfort.

As I eat, I stare at the scene, averting my eyes when the guard throws his glance in my direction.

I finish up and the waitress stops by with an invitation in her eyes as she whispers huskily, "Mr. Romanov. May I interest you in anything else?"

"Vodka. Make it a double." I say with disinterest and lift my phone, that is awash with incoming texts.

As I pretend to scroll through them, I am more interested in the scene at the table across from me as the two strangers carry on ignoring one another.

When my drink arrives, I nod toward a booth near the window that offers a better view of my fellow travelers, and the waitress places my drink on her silver tray and follows me over to it.

Once I settle in, I am happy with a different view because now I can see the woman herself, not her guard. She is wearing dark glasses and appears to be staring at the menu but I have an over-whelming sensation she is staring directly at me.

I raise my glass and her menu is quickly raised to cover her face, causing me to smirk. My senses never fail me, and it has almost become a game pitching my skills against my fellow humans.

I register everything about them. What they are wearing, carrying, and their mannerisms. I am a studier of people and I'm good at what I do. It's a hobby with me, usually enabling me to bring my enemies down.

Yes, Alexei Romanov didn't get his billions from sitting back and letting people in front of the line. I take what I want and use my competition's weaknesses against them. It's no different in my private life and it's become more of a game to me of proving I can win than wanting to keep my prize.

I love the chase, the intrigue, and the steal. Women who don't belong to me are fair game. I want what everyone else has and when they are mine, I don't want them anymore and there is something about that girl that makes me hope she's on my flight. It will pass the time, all twenty-three hours of it and when we land, I will leave a ruined soul behind me.

Yes, I really hope she is on my flight.

I keep my eyes on my prize for the next hour and follow them when the flight is called to the gate.

I tuck myself in behind them, several paces back and delight in gazing at her sexy ass as she sways in front of me.

Her guard is doing a bad job of remaining unobtrusive as he walks beside her, holding her bags in both hands, which in my mind is a fatal error. I always have one arm free to reach for my gun, knife, or just a man's throat if he gets in my way.

I almost pity her for the protection she has because it's doubtful she would stand any chance of survival if she was in danger. It makes me smile to myself because she is in danger. From me and my interest in her.

As we near the gate, they head to the front, anxious to be among the first to board and as I reach the woman checking our boarding passes, I whisper a word in her ear that causes the alarm to heighten on her face.

She nods at me gratefully as she waves me through and as I head to the window, I lean against the glass and stare at the young woman through the reflection. She is averting her face from the other passengers and staring at her phone, but there is something telling me she is studying me right back.

My phone buzzes and I'm interested to see the text from my assistant Gleb, and I wonder if I can really pull this one off.

The trouble is, I can't even refuse a challenge from myself and so I text back my reply and turn my attention to getting what I want — as always.

SERENA

That man. I can't tear my eyes away from him. He is something else. There is something so incredibly powerful about a man like him. His rugged good looks complement a body that appears to be made from sin. Jet black hair slicked back, revealing a handsome face that could grace any aftershave campaign. He is wearing a black polo shirt and jeans, a tan suede jacket making a casual statement. His expensive watch is one money can't, buy purely because there were only ten made in the entire world. I happen to know because my grandfather has one and delights in telling us the story.

A man of means and an attitude of arrogance. My favorite blend of rugged temptation. I have his interest and he has mine and I wonder if he's sitting anywhere near me.

"Excuse me, sir." I am so invested in my study of the stranger, I didn't notice the cops approaching.

"Is there a problem, officer?" I say sharply and Connor moves to stand in front of me, a statement that obviously doesn't go down well with the cops.

"Sir, please come with us." He says to Connor, who replies roughly, "Why?"

"We need to search you. Purely routine."

"Like fuck it is." I say angrily, and the cop merely nods respectfully. "It won't take long."

Connor is angry but realizes there is nothing he can do and turns to me and whispers, "Stay here. Talk to no one, look at no one and I'll be back before we board."

He thrusts the documents in my hands and whispers, "Just in case they board and I'm not back. Take your seat and wait for me."

I say angrily, "I'll call my grandfather. He will sort this out."

The cop shrugs. "Call who you like, madam. We won't take long."

I watch helplessly as they escort Connor from the gate and, as my hand hovers over my phone, I find myself delaying the call I promised. I'm not sure why, but my eyes flick to the window, and I notice the man has gone and for some reason a huge wave of disappointment hits me.

Then a sexy husky voice whispers behind me, "It appears that your guard was carrying drugs. Shocking when you think of his blatant disregard for airport security."

My heart beats erratically and yet my voice is calm as I reply, "We both know he is carrying nothing but a bag, Mr…"

"Romanov. Alexei Romanov, Miss…"

I ignore him and a shiver of expectation passes through me as his lips brush against my ear and he whispers, "It's a long flight to Australia to take alone."

"I'm not alone." I say, his breath against my skin causing me to shiver.

"I have a proposition for you."

"I'm not interested." I am aching to turn and stare at the stranger who is doing something strange to me inside. His voice is husky and loaded with promise as he whispers, "I think you are extremely interested. I think you are searching for an adventure. Aching to do something reckless and against the rules."

"You don't know anything about me, Alexei."

I turn and stare into the darkest eyes that are loaded with power, and it takes my breath away.

I know those eyes.

I live surrounded by them, but none excites me in the same way that these ones do. Up close, he is even more handsome. A rugged beauty that tells of hard beginnings. A real man. The kind of man I'm used to. A man who takes no shit and doesn't care about the consequences and I smile as I stare into those eyes and whisper, "It was you."

He raises his eyes with amusement and shrugs, not even bothering to deny it.

"You called the cops on my companion." I shake my head. "You're a wicked man, Alexei. I kind of admire those qualities."

"I thought you might."

We hear the announcement to board and Alexei glances at the exit.

"It appears your friend may be some time."

"Apparently so."

He leans forward and whispers, "It turns out I won't be traveling on this flight after all."

I hate that my heart crashes with disappointment, but I give nothing away and he whispers, "You have a choice. Board this flight, or my private jet that is waiting nearby."

"You're crazy." I stare at him in disbelief, and his eyes flash as he nods in agreement. "Crazy for adventure. What do you say, my mysterious woman? Go on an adventure with me or endure twenty-three hours of boredom alone."

He stares at me with the hottest look I have ever had directed my way that sends delicious flutters through my entire body.

I picture my grandfather and my brothers, their furious faces urging me to walk away from him. I picture my mother's shocked expression when I arrive in Sydney on a different flight, and I picture my one shot at adventure disappearing in a jet stream as I take the easy, safe option.

I grin. I'm not that girl. I'm not a Vieri by blood for nothing and the safer option is nowhere near as appealing as the one in front of me now.

In the extremely short time this man has captured my attention, I have experienced so many emotions I'm struggling to keep up. So, I lean forward and tiptoe to whisper in his ear, "I kind of like the idea of an adventure. Make it a good one."

He nods and reaches for my hand and as we walk to the exit, I have a feeling this is going to be one adventure I may never recover from.

CHAPTER 1

ALEXEI

*I*t doesn't take much to inform the staff of our decision and head to the exit. I'm aware the flight will be held up while they offload our bags, but that doesn't concern me. What does is passing the next twenty-three hours with a stranger. A pretty stranger who has impressed me with her sense of adventure.

As we head back the way we came, I carry her bag despite her insistence she can carry it herself.

"Non-negotiable," I say abruptly with a determination that causes her to raise her eyes and stare at me with a wry smile.

"I'm guessing you never take no for an answer, Alexei." she whispers in her slightly husky voice.

"It would be a foolish person who tries to deny me."

I shrug with the arrogance of a man who always gets what he wants, and she has proven no exception to that rule so far and as we stride along the walkway, I am impressed that she matches my speed perfectly.

Conversation is limited, which suits me because that is not what interests me about her. She will be a distraction for my flight, and that is all. When we reach Sydney, she will be handed over to whoever meets her, probably ruined and almost certainly broken. My interest in her will be a distant memory, and I will move on with my business.

I notice the crew moving toward us in the distance and it's obvious we escaped the flight just in time. If the call was any later, we would be boarding in around fifteen minutes and my depraved imagination would have to work with a more public venue in mind. Now I get to enjoy my passenger with no interruptions, and I am happy things have worked out so well—for me, anyway.

Something makes me study the crew a little closer as they head toward us, and there is one person I can't drag my eyes away from. Even from the distance they look familiar and my blood chills as I contemplate something that would have made that flight extremely interesting.

I pull my companion closer beside me and position us behind a woman with a very large suitcase and then, as the crew advance, I grab her hand and spin her before me on the moving walkway. My arms wrap around her as I lower my face to hers with a soft, "Play along princess, this is where it gets interesting."

As my lips dust hers, she whispers, "What is it?"

That statement alone impresses me because I thought she was the kind of girl who would be shocked by my sudden move. Instead, she correctly senses an ulterior motive and I whisper huskily, "I'll tell you in a minute."

I wrap my hand around the back of her head and as our lips touch, I kiss her softly, wishing like hell our first kiss was under different circumstances. I have no time to savor the delicious taste of forbidden fruit as I scan the face of the approaching flight attendant as she chats with the colleague by her side.

They move past without even a glance in our direction and as they leave, I release my captive and feel my blood churning.

I was right.

I quicken my pace and as I politely request to pass the couple in front, my companion is wise not to say a fucking word.

Gone is my playful intent and I have already shed my good mood. I am fucking raging inside because what the hell was Regina doing on that flight?

We move at a fast pace toward the private gates and as we reach the one assigned to my company, I waste no time in making the call that will clear up the mystery for me.

"Boss."

"Regina Silver."

I almost spit her name into the microphone.

"Find out why she was working my fucking flight to Sydney."

"Consider it done."

I cut the call, trusting Gleb to deal with this shit and as we pass the attendant manning the desk, I present my passport and say to my companion brusquely, "Passport."

She presents the document and the woman on the desk allows us to pass through and as we take the stairs, she almost has to run to keep up.

I am so preoccupied I ignore her completely and so am surprised when I hear an angry, "Stop right there!"

I turn and see the fierce expression on the girl's face as she drops her bag to the ground beside her. She is facing me with flashing blue eyes that I never appreciated the beauty of before as she sets her plump lips in an angry line and hisses, "What just happened and cut the bullshit?"

For a second, I can only stare because anger suits this woman well. Her chest is heaving, and her cheeks flushed, but it's those eyes that are mesmerizing. She glares at me from under her baseball cap and in this moment, I believe she could strike me dead from just a well-aimed word in my general direction.

I knew I was attracted to her, but that attraction is nothing to how I feel now as I stare at a goddess of war who unleashes the wild beast inside me. I can tell we will explode together, and it will be an experience I am unlikely to forget in a hurry.

All these emotions scramble my mind for the briefest second before I exhale sharply and nod back in the direction we came.

"The woman who passed us on the walkway."

"The one with the blonde hair chatting to the aloof one beside her."

She raises her eyes, and it makes me smile because it appears that I have underestimated my companion.

"Yes."

"What about her?" She asks coolly, but her eyes flash with a danger that excites me rather than alarms. I decide to test her resolve to its limits and lay out the facts, just so I can watch terror replace the anger in those beautiful eyes.

"That woman was an assassin."

"Dressed as a flight attendant."

She shakes her head. "How do you know?"

I'm surprised that her anger has been replaced by a completely different emotion than I thought. It appears that once again I have underestimated this astonishing woman because the emotion replacing anger is excitement.

"Regina Silver is a paid assassin who uses her job as cabin crew as a cover."

"And you know that because…"

She raises her eyes and shows no fear at all, causing me to laugh softly.

"Do you find that funny, Alexei?" She cocks her head to one side, and I nod.

"I'm amused. I can't deny it but to answer the questions you are lining up in your mind…"

I advance slowly toward her and whisper, "I have paid for her services several times."

My voice is smooth and slightly husky as I edge closer, holding her fierce gaze with mine as I whisper against her ear,

"She charges a flat fee to deal with unwanted problems. She is well known in the industry and so the question remains, who was her target?"

I tip her face to mine and growl, "I don't take kindly to surprises my little tiger and it wouldn't surprise me if I was in her sight, so forgive me if I'm a little distracted, but I want answers and fast."

The flicker of excitement in those soulful eyes momentarily blinds me and as her lips dust against mine, she whispers, "I kind of like danger, Alexei. It excites me."

"Is that so?"

I laugh softly against her lips and then she surprises me by lifting her hand and running her finger down my face, her nails scratching the rough skin before she grips my jaw and says huskily, "I don't get many chances to stretch my wings and fly, so I'm counting on you to make this memorable but just a word of warning before we go any further."

I stare into her eyes with a blank expression, my cool reserve kicking into play as I face her with zero emotion.

"You are warning—me?" I laugh softly and she smiles as she stares into my eyes with a smoldering expression of lust.

"Don't expect anything more than twenty-three hours of my time because when that aircraft lands, I *will* walk away, and you will never see me again."

She grins, her eyes flashing with excitement as she whispers huskily against my lips, "And what goes on in the sky, stays in the sky, honey, and I'm counting on you to make it one hell of a flight."

Before I can react, she reaches down and picks up her bag and shrugs.

"So what if someone is out to kill you? It may not be you they are after."

She drops me a sexy wink, which makes me laugh out loud and she nods in the direction we are heading. "So, show me to your private jet, Alexei, and I will be the judge if I am impressed or not."

I turn and walk away, hiding the broad smile on my face her words created. She didn't even flinch when I told her who Regina was, which me makes me wonder what world this tiger lives in. It's obvious she isn't your average passenger; her paid protection already alerted me to that. Now I just need her name and I will soon discover every delicious thing about her, and yet somehow, it's the mystery that's attracting me right now and knowledge can wait until I'm bored with playing the game.

CHAPTER 2

SERENA

*a*s I follow him, there is one thing I can't stop thinking about. How he tasted when he kissed me.

Despite the shocking statement about an assassin on our flight, that is all I can focus on.

He was so good. Like every dark wish I've ever had.

He is different from every man I have ever met and yet is also the same. He is familiar in a way that should repel me but at the same time he is home. I know men like him. I understand men like him and I live with men like him.

Is he mafia? Russian mafia? Everything points that way, but if he is, where are his guards? He could be an enforcer and takes care of his own shit. He certainly looks as if he can but there is a polished arrogance about the man which tells me he is in charge.

Yes, I know him because he is the man I have been searching for my entire life.

WE HEAD out of the terminal onto the tarmac, and I note a car waiting with a man standing beside the open door, his mirrored shades disguising his solemn expression and the alert way he scans the area tells me I was right.

Fucking mafia. I knew it.

He nods as Alexei approaches and doesn't even react when I join him and as we slide into the car, he slams the door and heads around to the front passenger seat.

I say nothing as the car heads toward the private area and as I stare out of the window, I note our original aircraft waiting patiently to leave. The hold is open, and the men are searching through the cases, which informs me that Alexei holds a certain kind of influence here.

I take it all in and, far from being afraid at what I'm doing, I'm impatient to get started.

We sit in silence as we head toward a sleek black jet with a silver insignia on the tail. I can't make it out and say with interest, "Is that your company logo?"

"You could call it that."

"What else would it be called? A logo's a logo."

I roll my eyes and he shrugs. "You are right, but you didn't listen to the whole sentence."

"Then explain." I turn to face him, and he smirks.

"You asked me if it was my company logo. It's my family one."

"Family, as in a coat of arms type of thing?"

I'm interested, and he shakes his head. "I am no aristocrat, tiger. What I am is a member of the Romanov family. A Russian family with strong ties to the motherland. We are one of the most feared families in Russia and yet we are not criminals. We own a business that nobody messes with, but we keep within the law – to a point." He winks and I say with curiosity, "What business?"

I'm intrigued, and he leans back and stares at me with a hard expression as he says evenly, "Mainly arms. We also own several banks, steel companies, oil refineries and deal in diamonds. Where there is money to be made, we are interested, and our empire is far reaching."

"Our?"

He nods. "I am one of several Romanov men. I choose to conduct my business in America, occasionally traveling on business. I have several brothers and cousins who prefer to work in their own chosen field. Mine is diamonds."

"Interesting." I stare at the jet that isn't far off the size of the one waiting to take us to Australia and I say with a smile, "Then I hope the problem has been fixed with your ride because I don't want to make this journey my last."

He laughs and I stare at him in surprise. That smile could set a convent alight. It completely transforms his rather stern features and as his face relaxes, it brings with it a beauty I never attributed to a man. The rough edges are softened and strangely compelling and I itch to run my fingers along his strong jaw. To gaze into his mysterious eyes and fall into his secrets, discovering what they are and deciding whether they are worth my time or not.

Alexei Romanov.

Why have I never heard of him before?

The car pulls up beside the incredible jet and as the door opens, we step out into the brilliant sunshine.

The steps are covered in a black carpet, and I roll my eyes.

"That's a little flash, if you don't mind me saying, and totally pointless."

"No, I don't mind you saying but your words hold no weight with me."

He turns and stares at me with a hard look of command that makes my knees almost buckle as he says harshly, "I don't give a fuck what you think about my choices and if want to act like an arrogant jerk with my money, I will."

Now it's my turn to laugh out loud and for a second he stares at me in much the same way I did at him.

Then a smile lights his eyes as he offers me his hand.

"I never did get the pleasure of your name."

STELLA ANDREWS

"No." I smile back at him as I take his hand and whisper, "I don't believe I offered it."

We enter the plane, but that is where the description ends. It's as if I have entered a fucking hotel and I stare in amazement at the interior of a palace in the sky.

"Wow! This is impressive. I knew I made the right decision."

I laugh as I gaze around me in wonder.

Alexei appears to be judging my response and I suppose I should play it cool, but this is a once in a lifetime experience and I say in awe. "I'm just surprised you were going to travel commercially."

"I have business to attend to. It always comes first."

"Of course."

I know a lot about that because my family is the same. Business always takes precedence, and I understand what he means.

I nod at the liveried attendant, who almost bows to the man by my side.

"Mr. Romanov. Your usual?"

"Not this time, Anton. I'll show my guest to her room and then I'll meet with Gleb."

"Of course, sir, follow me."

We start to follow him, and I whisper, "My room?"

I keep pace beside him and lower my voice. "You mean this really is a hotel? Wow again."

He shrugs. "It has many rooms. We travel long distances and comfort is the top priority. There is also a gym, a movie theater and a restaurant. If you are weary, I have a spa where a trained masseuse will attend to you and if you require any treatments, that can be arranged too."

"What do you do with your time on board?"

I'm mildly curious because, knowing the men in my family, business always takes over.

"I amuse myself."

He shrugs. "I work, play, eat and rest. It passes the time."

"Play?" That word alone causes my blood to heat because I'm guessing the kind of games this man likes to play and he nods, throwing a heated look my way with a soft, "If you want to play the game, I will show you how."

"Who says I don't know already?" I raise my eyes and he grins, that panty melting grin that gets me every time.

"You may not have played my favorite game, tiger."

"Then teach me." I fire back, loving the lust that heats his gaze as he directs it my way and I swear to God, every wish I ever had is being granted right now as he slides those eyes the length of my body and then back to my face and smirks, "Give me one hour and just for the record, you asked for it."

He turns away and I really should back away and fast because this man's games could ruin me. I may not leave this aircraft the same woman that entered it and I sincerely hope I don't. I am so bored with playing it safe. Bored of doing the right thing and searching for kicks that would send my grandparents to an early grave. Serena Vieri has been protected her whole life but even they didn't see this man coming and I am not going to waste this opportunity, whatever it involves.

CHAPTER 3

ALEXEI

I walk with my guest to her room and as we enter, I stare at the pretty space dressed in ivory silk with gold trim.

It's a room fit for a princess and, as always, money has not been spared in its creation. She stares around her with an eagerness that makes me smile. There have been many occupants of this room before, and all of them appreciate its decadence. She is no exception and I expect she will be no different from them.

Women who are faced with wealth on this grand scale soon lose their modesty and any fears they may hold. I have ruined many women in this room and all of them are grateful for it. She will be no different, and that almost saddens me. I *want* her to be different. Unexpected even. If she lies back and takes my shit, I will lose the growing respect I have for her. Her reaction to this room saddens me because it's just like all the others before her and so, with an inward sigh, I turn and say abruptly, "One hour. Enjoy your solitude while you can."

As I leave, it's in silence because she appears to have forgotten I'm here at all as she wanders deeper into the room and runs her hand over the silk edges and wallows in the delights my money can buy.

I close the door and head to meet my assistant with a growing sense of impatience. I thought she was a challenge. It appears I was wrong.

* * *

I FIND my assistant in the office where I usually spend a great deal of my flight. He is working on the computer and glances up as I enter.

"Alexei."

I sink down into the seat opposite the desk, motioning him to stay in my usual one and say darkly, "What have you got?"

"She was a last-minute replacement for a crew member who went sick last night. Standard procedure."

I'm not buying it and growl, "Who is her target?"

He types on the screen and the passenger manifest comes up, and he has highlighted several names already. He turns the screen to me, and I note mine is highlighted, along with a few other names in first class and a few in business.

"Any ideas?"

He shakes his head. "There is no word from our contacts, and her bank account in Switzerland is business as usual."

He brings up another screen and I read the entries on a bank statement in her name. He points to one that he highlighted dated two days ago for three hundred thousand dollars.

"This one is a ghost which tells me it's what we're looking for. An unknown number that traces into oblivion. Whoever is paying her doesn't want to be identified, which leaves us only one course of action."

"Is it arranged?" I'm asking a question I already know the answer to because Gleb is always ten steps ahead of me.

"Your brother Mikhail has promised to deal with it. She won't make it out of her hotel room."

"Anything else I should know?"

He shakes his head.

"The engineering problem has been dealt with and passed all the checks. Your meeting is on schedule in Sydney, and your itinerary is unchanged."

"What about my guest? Is there any news about her identity?"

I'm mildly interested, even though it means nothing, and Gleb nods. "Mae Grayson. An heiress from San Diego heading to Australia to her mother's house in Vaucluse."

I hear his words, but something about them isn't ringing true. I expected more than this and I lean forward and growl, "Dig deeper. I'm not buying it."

"Why?" He stares at me in surprise, and I shake my head. "I don't ignore my instincts. I want a full background check ran on this Mae Grayson and if she is who her passport says she is, I'm not worthy of my family name."

Gleb smiles softly. "Understood."

"Is everything set for the meeting with Stoner?" I say as an aside, and he nods. "He won't know what hit him, the arrogant prick."

It makes me laugh because Gleb has a burning hatred for that man. Mainly because he dismisses him as the hired help and refuses to deal with anyone but me. Little does he know that Gleb is the oil that runs my machine and without him, it would grind to a halt. You anger my main man at your peril because he will do you no favors and Joseph Stoner needs us far more than we need him, and he knows it.

I try not to dwell on the man who irritates the shit out of me, but he has contacts in Australia I can only get to through him. He is the front man for a shit load of diamonds and the supply is limitless and a very good price. Stoner takes his cut as the middleman, which drives up the price. I am impatient to cut him out because Gleb is right to be irritated by him.

Stoner wallows in his own self-importance and treats anybody who meets with him as an imbecile. He knows that his contacts rely on him and prefer to conduct their business this way. Subsequently, he calls the shots and I fucking hate doing business with him, but I need his diamonds more than I need him put in his place.

Gleb's attention returns to his screen, and it amuses me how he disregards my presence, as if I'm merely an irritant. He is a workaholic with no private life to speak of, allowing only enough time to sleep, shower and eat and then he is back to running my empire and providing me with the information I need. He has no time for hierarchy, it only gets in the way of his work, and I am happy to let him. I don't stand on ceremony anyway and I never have.

I make to head back to my guest but decide to settle in first. I could use a shower and a change of clothes and so I head to my own room instead.

As I step inside, I love the dark charcoal walls and gray silk that awaits me. Subdued lighting illuminates only the parts I want it to and the wood paneling that is painted a similar color affords a masculinity that settles my soul.

I head to the silver tray set on the table and grip the bottle of vodka in one hand and take a huge mouthful, swilling it around my mouth, savoring the bite and then swallowing it, loving the burn as it coats me inside.

I tear off my clothes and move to the walk-in shower and stand under the powerful jets as they soak away my weariness. Seeing Regina has unsettled me. I live with constant threats to my life, but I never expected one from her. She has been a guest of mine on several occasions, and I feel betrayed somehow. If I was her intended target, I am pissed because it means she has no loyalty to me at all, even though I have paid her many times over for her business and fucked her for fun. Fucking women. They always betray you in the end when somebody with more money and prospects comes knocking.

I towel off and stare at my reflection with a sense of growing anger. Women! They will be my ruin because I couldn't keep away if I tried. Just the fact there's one already waiting for me who took zero persuasion to bring her here affords me a hatred for the easy way they spread their legs and take what they can. I have never met a woman who doesn't want what I can offer them, and it appears my little heiress is no exception.

I pull on my silk pants and leave my chest bare and as I run my fingers through my wet hair, I set my mind to bastard. She will provide entertainment for a few hours and then she can sleep the rest of the way to Australia before I set her free to ruin another man's soul.

I wonder if she knows what I am capable of. I'm guessing she hasn't got a fucking clue, otherwise she wouldn't be here now. That thought alone makes me smile and as I set off to find my little tiger, I am preparing to rip out her claws—one by one.

CHAPTER 4

SERENA

*A*s soon as he leaves, I waste no time in surveying my surroundings. It's a pretty room, no doubt to delight his usual guests, and it is impressive. I'll give him that. I stare at the bed with derision, picturing the multiple occupants that have undoubtedly been here before me. I already realize Alexei is a player. He gets his kicks from wild adventure and I kind of admire that about him. However, it's his recklessness that causes me to view him in an entirely different way and I wonder if he has ever faced a challenge quite like me before.

I doubt it. Men like him prefer their women willing, compliant and gullible. Vacuous blondes, pretty brunettes and seductive women with dark hair and soulful eyes. I'm guessing he has enjoyed a cornucopia of women in the past and I would be a fool not to enjoy his attention to pass the time. However, first we need to set a few ground rules in place and if he doesn't agree, it's game over already.

I drop my holdall onto the bed and unzip it, smiling as I picture the one I brought through security safely back in the car where it came from.

As I pull out the revolver, I make certain it's loaded and then find my lipstick and sweep it generously across my fading lips. I am now armed with more than just a weapon because I hide behind my war paint in fear of being exposed. I let nobody in for a very good reason. They want the mafia princess, not the woman.

I lean back against the pillows and contemplate my life. I have never known any different. Guarded, cosseted and loved too hard. Any guys I dated never make it back for a second one. My brothers are snarling guard dogs who adopt a zero-tolerance policy where I am concerned.

The odd guard I seduced couldn't cope with the pressure, and my sexual education has been severely neglected. The only fun I ever had was when I managed to dodge the guards on a night out and lure an unsuspecting guy into my web. I am so desperate to discover what everyone but me knows it seems, which is why I seized my chance when Alexei offered it to me.

I'm aware of what he wants. It's obvious and I wouldn't be here now if he didn't believe I was a sure thing. Men like him disgust me, but it's a man like him I need right now. But first I have my rules that he would be a fool to refuse.

The gun is underneath the pillow, and my mind is set. When he returns, I will offer him a choice and it will be interesting to see how he reacts to that.

An hour later, as promised, the door opens without even a knock, and I stare at him as he enters. He is naked from the waist up, his huge chest inked, his abs dancing before my lustful eyes. The silk pants hang low on his hips, offering me a tantalizing glimpse of what he can offer me, and his dark eyes find mine and glitter with depravity, causing me to whisper huskily, "You like to make a statement."

"Is that what you think?"

He prowls into the room like a black panther, and I sense my claws sharpening as he advances.

"I thought you would have settled in by now."

He casts his lustful gaze over my body, still dressed in my black leggings and hoody, and I shrug.

"I have. Thank you for asking."

He stares at me with a hard expression and says roughly, "We both know why I asked you to travel with me. I'm guessing you're a little nervous about that."

"You think I'm nervous?"

I laugh out loud. "You don't intimidate me, Alexei. Yes. In answer to your question, I know exactly why you invited me to travel with you. I'm curious though."

"About what?" He sits on the edge of the bed, and I shrug. "How were you going to play it on board the commercial jet? I am intrigued."

"It's easy." He smirks. "I always travel on airlines with privacy screens. This airline does it well and the seats are more like rooms. I intended on slipping inside your 'room' when the lights were dimmed and fastening the do not disturb sign on the door. We would enjoy our own private party, and I'm guessing you would have loved every minute of it."

"That's an arrogant statement to make, Alexei."

I shake my head. "I'm disappointed in you."

He arches his brow.

"Disappointed?"

I nod, stretching out with a sigh.

"I could be anyone. You could have invited another assassin into your private space, and nobody would ever know."

"Only my staff, or have you forgotten I'm unable to operate this jet single-handedly and fuck you at the same time?"

"Fuck me, Alexei?"

He leans forward and yet before he can reach out and touch me, I pull out my gun and aim it right between his eyes.

To his credit, he just stares at me with a wry smile on his lips and I whisper, "So, back off and I'll tell you what is going to happen."

He leans back and appears almost amused as I hold the gun in place and whisper, "Just so you know, I *am* a sure thing. I'm not interested in your wealth, trying to trap you, or becoming your girlfriend."

He fixes me with an increasingly lustful stare, and I say huskily, "I only want your body. I want you to show me how good sex can be and leave me with a memory I will enjoy revisiting when you are far away from me. When we land, I never want to see you again, and you will ignore me if our paths cross."

I smile sweetly. "I am your worst nightmare wrapped up in every dream you ever had, Alexei. I am *not* your happily ever after and you are not mine. If you try to contact me after this flight, I will deny ever knowing you and take steps to remove you from my life. Do we have a deal?"

I'm surprised when he moves quickly and his strong hand wraps around my wrist, squeezing it hard so the gun shakes in my grasp. His eyes flash as he tears the gun from my hand with his other one and slides it across the room to the door. Then he grips both my wrists and pushes me back onto the bed and kicks my legs apart, pinning me down and whispers against my ear, "I agree to your terms, my little tiger. Strangers suits me just fine."

His lips crash onto mine and this time it's not soft. This time it's angry and yet weirdly I prefer it to the first one.

His hands press against my skin and his teeth bite down on my lower lip and yet I don't struggle. That's not what this is about. It's about getting something I've wanted for a long time now and he will fulfill the fantasy perfectly.

CHAPTER 5

ALEXEI

*T*hank God for that. I was right; she is living up to every desire I had and far from being angry about the gun pointed at my head; I loved it. The way she looked at me with a mixture of lust and hate made me hard and I would have died happy if she had taken it that far.

Now, as she lies beneath me, she kisses me back with mounting passion, and I drown in her power. She is the first woman who has ever played me at my own game, and I love it.

Her body is flush against mine and I'm impatient to feel her skin on skin, but that pleasure can wait. This is about setting the rules and now she has played her hand. It's time to play mine.

I pull back and love her swollen lips and eyes that are heavy with lust as she gazes at me and I pull her up to face me and whisper, "I agree to your rules. Now for mine."

"I'm listening." She whispers against my lips, and I grin and pull her beside me, securing her wrists behind her back with my hand.

"We will use each other for pleasure on the journey and, at the other end, walk away."

"That was my condition."

She grins and I nod. "Then we are of the same mind."

I smile into her eyes, loving how they draw me in deeper and whisper, "I will use your body and make you do things you never believed possible. You will be uncomfortable about some of them, but you will love them all the same."

"I'm intrigued—go on."

The light in her eyes tells me I've met my perfect woman and I smirk. "We spend the next twenty-three hours together and enjoy the experience. That's all I ask. Keep an open mind and enjoy the ride."

"Okay." She smiles with excitement, which makes me laugh.

I cup her cheek in my free hand and gaze into her eyes and whisper, "So, how does a woman get a gun through security? Just for future reference."

"I didn't." She grins impishly.

"That bag is now safely back at home. This bag..." She nods to the one on the floor. "I picked this one up in Duty Free. It's amazing what people leave lying around, you know."

She grins and there is one big red flag waving at me because I was right to trust my instincts.

"Who are you and don't say Mae Grayson, because I simply don't believe you?"

She laughs out loud.

"If I told you, it would strip away the fun."

I shake my head. "I will find out. It's only a matter of time."

"It will make no difference." She sighs. "I am nobody, Alexei. Just a woman heading off to visit her mom. You won't see me again and if my family discover I was here with you, I apologize about that but well, I have a feeling you can handle yourself and as this plane has taken off there is nothing you can do to avoid it."

She shrugs. "Like I said, you disappoint me, Alexei, because you really should know who you are dealing with before you bring them into your life."

Her words should alarm me but I'm the arrogant bastard who believes he is invincible and so I rest my lips against hers and hiss, "Then bring it on, tiger and if I'm going down, it's on you first."

The way her eyes widen and her chest heaves scores me a minor victory because whoever she is, she's here now. In my arms and preparing to be ruined by me and if anyone should be afraid right now, it's her.

I move in for another leisurely kiss, but she averts her head. "Not here."

"Why not?"

"Because I will not be considered another notch on this bed post."

She turns those incredible eyes to mine, and they flash as she whispers, "I'm guessing you have fucked many companions in this bed. I will not be one of them. I deserve better."

"So, what did you have in mind?"

"A tour of this incredible plane would be a start a guess and after I could make my decision based on having all the facts."

"Then consider me your tour guide, tiger."

I reach out and take her slender hand in mine and pull her up to join me.

As we leave the cabin, she laughs softly. "Do you always prowl around half naked?"

"No."

I shrug. "I'm sparing your blushes and pulled on my pants this time."

I wink and she laughs softly, an act that completely changes her. I stare in amazement as her features soften and transform before my eyes. Her eyes sparkle and her white teeth gleam as she relaxes for the first time since we met.

Now she has ditched the baseball cap, her hair shines like polished metal and hangs low down her back like a sheet of black silk. I am itching to run it through my fingers but resist for my own sanity because touching this woman has become an irresistible urge that I am losing the battle of.

"What is your name, pretty tiger?" I must know because Mae doesn't suit her at all.

"Okay." She shrugs. "I'll give you that at least. It's Serena."

"That's better." I squeeze her hand. "I like it."

"Thank you." She grins, and it makes me smile. To be honest, everything about this woman makes me smile, even when she held a gun to my head. It makes me wonder about my reaction to her. Since she walked into the airport lounge, I was fascinated by her. A slight figure dressed in black, trying hard not to draw attention to herself. I'm guessing she could light up a dark room because she couldn't deflect attention away from her if she tried.

We head toward the gym and as I open the door, she turns to me with an excited gasp. "You weren't kidding. This is impressive."

"It helps pass the time. Not only for me, but my fellow travelers too."

She spins around and raises her eyes. "The men you surround yourself with?"

"Of course."

"What about women? Do they figure in your life at all?"

I shrug. "They do, but not on my security team. Women work for me in my business. Some are managers, some directors, but my security team are ex special forces and there aren't that many women I can call on to fill the roles."

"So, you don't only use women to satisfy your physical urges."

"No." I peer at her closely. "What about you, Serena? Do you have a high-powered job that hands men their balls for breakfast?"

I love how she throws her head back and laughs and I find myself staring. She is so beautiful. Self-assured, unafraid, and adventurous. A wild spirit much like me and I will be disappointed if she turns out to be just like the rest of the women I have entertained in my bed.

They are mainly just interested in money, their next surgery and snagging a billionaire. I kind of think this woman is better than that and I'm intrigued by her answer.

She sits astride one of the benches and gazes up at me with an allure I am struggling hard not to react to.

"I am expected to join my family business."

"So, you are an heiress."

I'm a little disappointed about that, and she grins.

"I can tell you have been researching your guest. Nice try."

I sit astride the bench beside her and raise my eyes. "So, I am wrong."

"No. You got that right, but unlike most pampered daughters, I am expected to pay dearly for my position."

For a second her eyes cloud and I note the bitterness in them, and she shakes her head and says somewhat sadly, "I have money. More than I can spend. I have a family who love me, too hard as it happens. Then I have a future. A complicated uncertain future that is mine to determine up to a point."

"So why the pain in your eyes, little one? Many would be happy with that."

She shrugs. "I didn't say I wasn't a spoiled bitch."

It makes me laugh. "I wouldn't have said that."

"I expect you thought it, though." She shakes her head.

"I am as it happens, but right at this moment, I'm a little lost both physically and mentally. I am struggling to find the woman in me and decide what it is she lost somewhere along the way."

"Is that why you're visiting your mom?" I enquire, and she nods, a wistful expression in her eyes.

"Well remembered. Yes, mom left years ago because my father, well, I won't sugar coat this, but he was a bastard and cheated on her."

She stares at me with a hurt expression, causing me to reach for her hand, which surprises me more than anything.

Why do I even care?

"I don't need your sympathy, Alexei, I just need your wild spirit. It was the reason I agreed to your request. For the first time in my life, I was free to make my own decision. There was nobody standing by my side preventing me and it felt liberating."

She stares at me with an intense look of longing that I know isn't for me but what I can give her, and it moves me. Not a lot does, but right in this moment she's vulnerable, which makes her a lot more appealing to me.

"I can do liberation, tiger." I grin and she laughs softly. "I'm counting on it."

I tug her sharply toward me, so she falls from the bench onto my lap, and I grasp her glorious hair, loving how soft it feels in my iron fist.

I stare into her incredible eyes that are flashing with excitement and whisper against her lips, "I want to be everything you have been searching for Serena, for twenty-three hours of your life. I want to teach, to corrupt and to delight. I want to ruin, and I want to destroy. I will reach in and drag the woman out of you, and we will leave as strangers."

"What about you, Alexei?"

She pulls back and studies me with an interested expression.

"Me?" I shrug. "What you see is what you get."

"I doubt it."

She runs her red painted fingernail down my chest and whispers, "There must be a reason why you seek sex with strangers. The forbidden, the unobtainable, and the desire to take what you want. What are you missing in your life that makes you so reckless?"

I close my eyes and take a deep breath because the hell I'm unlocking any of my secrets to her. I feel her thumb pressing against my lips and her soft breath in my ear as she whispers,

"What are you hiding from, Alexei? Why aren't you living a conventional life and take risks with your safety?"

I open my eyes to find her staring into them and I say huskily, "Because when you have everything that money can buy, you move onto what it can't. That is more valuable to me. Not having control over something is a hunger inside me that I feed off, but is never sated. I love the risks involved, the sense of the unknown and the euphoria when I get what I want. Then it ceases to be important anymore and I move on to the next challenge. It's an addiction that will never be conquered. I am my own worst enemy and only I can defeat the monster in me."

"Do you want to?"

She raises her eyes and I shake my head and chuckle. "Not right now. I am having too much fun to even try."

She laughs out loud, and I stare at a beauty I certainly wasn't expecting, and it strikes me that I have never met a woman like Serena before. One that is both beautiful and intelligent, with a wild spirit to match my own. She really couldn't give a fuck and that is a quality I admire in any man or woman.

This could be a memorable trip and maybe, just maybe, I will ask for an extension of our time together, despite what I said.

CHAPTER 6

SERENA

I really like Alexei Romanov. He is the first man I have ever opened up to like this and I suppose it's because for the first time I am free of my family. There are no guards listening to report back to my grandfather. I can say anything I like, and he knows shit about my life. I feel liberated, and it's a powerful emotion to deal with.

I *want* to be ruined by him. I doubt he will break me. That's been done countless times and the fragile pieces are glued back together with wisdom and a desire not to let it happen again. I'm in no doubt at all that he *could* break me but only if I let him. That is why twenty-three hours is all this will be. Long enough to make a fantastic memory and short enough to do minimum damage. It's perfect.

As I sit on his lap, I have an incredible urge to touch him. Just seeing his hard, toned body is a serious aphrodisiac and the dark, flashing eyes that strip my breath from inside me leave me panting for more of his dark attention.

I slide my fingers through his hair and love how he stares at me with a thousand promises of what he will do to me. This is what I want—what I need, and I thank God he was a passenger on my flight.

"So, what happens now?"

I whisper against his lips, and he says huskily, "We continue the tour."

"Of course."

I slide off his lap and stand, his hand entwined in mine as we head back the way we came.

THIS TIME we reach a movie theater and I gaze around with delight at the luxurious couches set in front of a huge screen, the red walls padded, and the lighting subdued.

As I settle into one of the couches, I stretch out with contentment.

"This is paradise. You certainly know how to travel in style, Alexei."

He drops down beside me and then rolls on top of me, pinning me to the couch as he kicks my legs apart.

"This is a perfect room for more than just watching movies." He says huskily and I gasp as his lips press against my neck and he bites down softly.

"It is."

I shiver as his rough hand inches under my hoody and slides across my skin like pebbles on sand. My whole body is standing to attention, desperate for more, and I groan as he presses soft kisses on my neck and cups my breast in his hand, flicking my nipple, causing delicious shivers to pass through my body.

I am panting with lust as he presses in harder, his huge erection straining against the silk of his pants and I moan as he rubs it against the thin fabric separating us and he whispers, "What will it be, tiger? Is this the right place?"

"No."

I gasp as a huge bolt of longing shoots through me, and he says softly, "Then we should move on to the next location."

As he pulls me up, I curse my stubborn streak because right in that moment, I wanted him more than air.

We leave the movie theater and head to another room that is filled with people, causing me to blink in surprise. It's a restaurant of sorts, with tables set around a huge space with white tablecloths draped over them. The tables are full of men, chatting and drinking, and they don't even gaze in our direction at all as we move through the tables to a vacant one set at the end.

Alexei holds out a chair and I sit, grateful for the comfort it brings as my legs still haven't recovered from his assault on my senses.

As he drops down into the seat in front of me, a waiter appears with two menus.

"Good afternoon, sir, madam."

He hands me the menu and I resist giggling because this is surreal. I stare out of the window at the clouds we fly among, and the sun lights the top of the wing, reminding me reality is just below us.

Alexei pours us both a glass of wine that is nestled inside a bucket on a stand beside the table and as I lift the cool sparkling glass, he touches his to mine.

"To wild adventure." He says with a grin, and I nod. "I'll second that."

The wine is as delicious as my companion and as soon as I make my food selection, the waiter retreats, leaving us to stare at one another across the table.

"This beats first class." I say, gazing around me with admiration, and he nods.

"It's the only way to travel."

"Yet you were prepared to slum it in first class with the peasants. Why?"

I'm curious about that. "Why not just delay your meeting?"

"Because business comes above my comfort." He shrugs, sipping the wine.

"Oh yes, the business."

"Oil?" I tip my head to one side, and he nods.

"Oil, diamonds, and steel. I dabble in it all."

He sets the glass down and stares at me with interest. "So, continue your story, little one. What is your family business?"

There it is. The million-dollar question and for some reason, I'm done with pretending. It's as if I can trust him, I don't know why and so I take a deep breath and say sadly, "Drugs, extortion, prostitution and gambling, to name just a few."

"Mafia?" He raises his eyes and I nod miserably. "That's the word."

To my surprise, he doesn't even blink and just raises his glass to mine and whispers, "That doesn't surprise me."

"Good."

We take another sip and then the waiter appears with a salad of seafood for each of us that looks incredible.

Alexei says with pride. "I have a Michelin star chef who travels with me. This is when my money counts for something amazing."

He grins as I stare at the food in wonder. "You are very lucky, although my grandmother's cooking is hard to beat."

"Tell me about your family." He says conversationally, and I'm guessing he is only being polite.

"My grandparents raised me and my two brothers when my parents split up. My father was more interested in his latest mistress and feathering his own nest to be concerned about the one he abandoned."

"That surprises me," he says, shaking his head.

"Why?"

"Because the mafia is big on family. I understand how it works and to go against your own doesn't lead to a healthy life."

"You're right about that." I shrug, loading up my fork with the delicious food.

"My brother murdered him."

I place the food in my mouth and stare at Alexei's reaction to that and as he lifts his own food to his mouth, it disguises an amused grin.

"Did that shock you?" I'm curious, and he shakes his head.

"He probably deserved it."

That makes me laugh and then say, "You should be shocked, repelled even."

"Why?" He shrugs. "I'm guessing it was done for a very good reason. I don't judge things before I know the facts."

I'm impressed, loving how easy he is to talk to, and I add.

"He ordered a hit on the entire family. He had to go."

He leans forward and stares at me with concern.

"A hit."

I shrug. "Your tale of the assassin on the flight wasn't that shocking to me. My family deal with shit like that every day of their lives. There is always someone wanting to take us down and who knows the target may even have been me."

I don't like the sudden urgency in his eyes as he stares past me and raises his hand.

Suddenly, the easy atmosphere has been replaced, and a man appears beside us almost immediately.

"Gleb." Alexei addresses him and waves toward me. "This is Serena. She may have been the intended target. Call Mikhail and inform him."

Gleb turns to me and his enigmatic expression hides what he's thinking as he says bluntly, "Serena, what is your last name?"

I can feel their eyes burning into me and know the game is up. If anything, it's in my interests because it appears they want to help, so I say with a slight shake of my head.

"Vieri."

I don't miss the look they share before Gleb leaves as quickly as he came.

I almost can't look at Alexei because that one name has blown away the easy atmosphere we created like a grenade tossed into the room.

"Serena." His hard voice commands me to look up and I'm shocked when I see the fire burning in his eyes as he reaches for my hand.

"Why didn't you tell me earlier?"

"What difference would it have made?" I say roughly, hating the way my life settles around me like a well-worn cloak, keeping everyone out as usual. It's as if the chains are snapping back in place and I am a prisoner once again. The tears burn my eyes as I watch the freedom I had disappearing in the jet stream and my heart is heavy as I accept my fate.

"It makes no difference to me, to us or to this situation."

He says softly, lifting my hand to his lips and kissing it tenderly. It surprises me as his eyes burn into mine and he whispers huskily, "It all makes sense now. I can see the whole picture and far from tainting it, it has only made it more beautiful to me."

"Why?" I'm shocked and he smiles softly. "Because now I understand you and with knowledge comes power."

"Over me?" His words irritate me, and he laughs out loud.

"No, Serena. It helps me make decisions that benefit you. You see, when Regina makes it to her hotel room in Sydney, she will have a visitor waiting for her. My brother Mikhail is on hand to extract the information we need. If she was ordered to carry out the hit on you, he will discover who ordered it. Then we can deal with the problem, leaving you free and safe to live another day. That is what we do. Safety always comes first, and you can sleep well knowing we have your back."

I'm touched and whisper, "Why would you help me?"

"Because we live the same life, little one."

He kisses my hand and stares into my eyes, and it's seducing me more than any touch or promise of freedom. "We are the same, my little tiger. We live the same life and understand the beauty and the evil it holds. I understand you because I *am* you to an extent. You disguise your identity to afford yourself freedom. Who you are changes nothing. We will go there anyway."

He winks, and it causes me to laugh, the chains dropping as if his words were a magic key.

With him, I am Serena Vieri, but I am also free. This is what I wanted, *he* is what I wanted, and it appears that sometimes dreams can come true.

CHAPTER 7

ALEXEI

$\mathcal{W}$e finish our meal with an easy familiarity. Despite being strangers a few hours ago, it's as if I've known her forever. As soon as I discovered her real identity, I understood. Mafia is something I have lived with my entire life because we are only one side step away from that. The Romanovs may not bear the title of Bratva, but we operate under the same rules, and some may say we are more deadly because of it.

Outwardly respectable and inwardly rotten to the core. Yes, I know Serena Vieri and have done since I first drew breath.

She appears pre-occupied, and I say softly, "What's troubling you, little one?"

"Is it that obvious? I need to adjust my mask." She smiles, and it's like a well-aimed dart to my heart. As the sun shines through the window, it surrounds her in majesty. Her eyes sparkle and the shine on her hair glows, making her almost ethereal. I am used to beautiful women accompanying me, sleeping with me, and decorating my arm, but I am *not* used to a woman like her. There is something so incredibly different about her, and I wonder if it's because of who she is.

"Tell me what you're thinking?" For some reason, I need to

know the whole of her and if anything is upsetting my guest, it upsets me too.

She sighs and replaces the fork, pushing her plate to one side.

"I think you're wrong about me, Alexei."

"In what way?"

"That I was the target."

"Why?" I raise my eyes and she exhales sharply.

"I was traveling under a pseudonym. We always do. A different one every time. Today I am Mae Grayson, my passport hot off the press. Nobody but my immediate family knew of this until the morning I left. The guards are kept ignorant unless they need to know. Connor was the only guard who was informed, and he only discovered it at the airport."

"Then it was someone else. That shouldn't be troubling you. It may be me, anyway."

"Probably." She laughs softly, but I can tell she is upset about something due to the dimming light in her eyes.

"There is still a but?"

I state and she nods, lifting those incredible eyes to stare at me with a hard expression.

"If it was me, we have a big problem."

"Because…" I raise my eyes and she sighs heavily.

"It means that one of my immediate family arranged it."

"I see."

I lean back and think about what she said. It's a possibility because even her own father ordered a hit on her, so I say carefully, "Who are we talking about?"

"I don't even want to imagine it could be any of them." She says sorrowfully and I say gently, "Business comes first. Detach your emotions and think clearly."

She nods, and I'm happy to see a little of the fire return to her expression.

"My grandparents and two brothers. Mom, of course, she knows I am coming, and I expect Stoner."

My ears prick up.

"Stoner?"

"My stepfather for want of a better word."

She shakes her head with distaste. "For some reason, mom loves him. I've always found him to be a fool."

"Then we agree on another thing."

I raise my glass to her, and she says with astonishment,

"You know him?"

I nod. "He is the man I am meeting with. My business in Australia if you like. He is the middleman to a diamond operation I am keen to do business with and they only negotiate through him."

I chuckle, "Gleb shares your opinion on the man. You have that in common at least."

"Then he's a good judge of character."

She looks concerned.

"Why would he want me dead, though? It doesn't make sense."

"No, but if it was him, we will soon find out."

"I guess." She glances up as the waiter appears with two plates of beef wellington, dauphinoise potatoes and steamed vegetables.

He produces a bottle of the finest red wine and pours two large glasses before retreating as silently as he came.

Serena smiles and sniffs appreciatively.

"Perhaps you should introduce me to your chef. When I've finished with you, I may run away with him."

She grins as I say with amusement. "You could try, but he prefers Gleb."

"No way."

Her eyes are wide, and I shrug. "I share your disbelief. Gleb is in love with business, and I'm surprised they find the time to be together."

"At least someone is happy, I suppose."

She lifts her cutlery, more intent on sampling the food than making further conversation with me and as I eat, I

watch her, taking in every detail of her pretty face. Her beautiful, wicked, soul shattering face that will be forever
imprinted on my memory. Yes, I realized there was something
incredible about this woman when I first set eyes on her. I
must remember to thank God for delivering her to my certain
brand of evil.

* * *

WE FINISH our meal and decide against dessert, and as we leave
the restaurant, she says with a soft smile. "Where next?"

"Perhaps you would like to compliment the chef and check
him out at the same time."

I raise my eyes and she laughs. "That sounds like a plan."

We walk toward the galley hand in hand, and it feels nice. A
simple act that I never appreciated the pleasure of before.

As we reach it, the aroma hits us as soon as we open the door
and she gasps, "Okay, it's official. You have ruined me, Alexei.
How can I ever travel another way again?"

It makes me laugh as she heads into the galley, and I introduce
her to Marcel, the Italian chef. Serena speaks to him in fluent
Italian, and he is obviously happy to oblige and for a moment I
watch as they move around the space as he points out several
things, occasionally stopping to sample some of his work and
discussing the merits of the ingredients he uses.

I love watching her as she listens with interest to what he says
and interjects, no doubt with suggestions from her grandmother's vast knowledge.

I lean against the wall and relish my uninterrupted study of
her because there appears to be nothing I don't like or admire
about this woman.

They finally stop talking and as she heads my way, her face is
lit with pleasure, and I shake my head. "Obviously, food is the
way to your heart."

She nods. "Or I could have arranged to run away with Marcel."

"You wouldn't get very far."

I nod toward the window. "Unless you have a death wish."

"Maybe I do."

She shrugs and for some reason her words sadden me. I lift her face to mine and whisper, "You have everything to live for and if I get my way, you will live a long and happy life."

"By terminating the contract." She shakes her head. "It will soon be replaced by another. It's an impossible mission that I won't hold you to."

She nods toward the door.

"Where next?"

As I take her hand, there really is only one place I want to be right now, but there is business to attend to first and what I have in mind could ruin everything.

* * *

THE NEXT ROOM we stop at is my office. There are many men working at desks, and I notice Gleb tapping into a computer in the corner. I stop by his desk and speak in Russian, which angers her because she taps me on the shoulder and says, "Don't be rude. If you want to keep secrets, do it when I'm not around."

"Says the woman who had a private conversation in Italian with her new love interest." I raise my eyes and Gleb grins as I say evenly. "I was asking him to check out Stoner if you must know."

"You mean you haven't already. You really do need to learn to investigate who you are doing business with."

She rolls her eyes, causing Gleb to grin wider and as we pass, she drops him a wink that he rewards with a broad smile.

She follows me in and perches on the edge of the desk and says with interest. "I like your office."

"You like my office?" I shake my head. "The least impressive room on this aircraft has impressed you more than anything else."

She nods. "Because it's part of you. The other places were communal ones. This space is filled with your personality and your scent."

"My scent?" I grin. "Are you saying I smell, Serena?"

"I am."

She crooks her finger summoning me, and as I stand before her, she leans in and presses a light kiss to my chest before inhaling deeply and groaning.

"I love your scent, Alexei. If I could bottle it, I would."

Just feeling her lips on my skin causes the blood to rush to my cock and with a low growl I pull her head up and leaning down, kiss her soft lips with a hunger that is only increasing the more time I spend with her.

She tastes of wicked delight, and I never realized how addictive it was.

She cups my hard cock through the fabric and whispers, "It appears you are getting impatient."

I bite down on her neck, causing her to moan softly, and I whisper, "I could say the same to you."

I make to lift her hoody and she wriggles out from my grasp and faces me with her eyes shining. Her heightened color reveals how much I affect her, and she gasps, "Not here. I want to visit your bedroom, Alexei, because if this room smells of you, that room must be paradise."

It makes me laugh, but then, as always, business comes first and so with a sigh, I point to the phone on my desk.

"I'm sorry about this tiger, but we need to call home first."

"I don't understand." She appears nervous and I say with a sigh. "It's the respectful thing to do because your family must be worried. They will know you weren't on that flight and your guard will be paying the price for that."

"I guess."

Her eyes drop and she sighs heavily.

"I'll call my grandfather. He will call the dogs off."

"No."

"No?"

She faces me with fire in her eyes and I smirk, "*I* will call your grandfather."

"Why?"

"Because it is respectful."

"Whatever." She turns away and I can tell she is hating this. Her reality has entered fantasy, and she is fighting against it.

I lift the phone and Gleb says, "Don Vieri for you, sir."

The next voice I hear is one that reeks of power.

"Alexei, it appears you have something of mine."

"Good afternoon, Don Vieri."

Serena looks up with burning emotion in her eyes as she hears her grandfather's name.

"Sir, with respect, we have a problem."

"We have a problem?" He laughs softly. *"I accept that you have a problem, Mr. Romanov, but I fail to see how that affects my organization."*

I take my seat and prepare to deliver the news.

"There was a paid assassin on Serena's flight, one I recognized having used her services myself. We must face the possibility she was there for your granddaughter."

"Impossible." He says in a rough whisper. *"Serena's safety is my top priority, and nobody was aware she was traveling."*

I take a deep breath. "I hope you're right, sir. My brother is waiting for the assassin and will soon discover the identity of her target. In the meantime, I wanted to assure you that Serena is safe, and no harm will come to her under my protection."

"Your protection." He laughs softly. *"We both understand the outcome of any harm coming to my granddaughter, Mr Romanov, but I appreciate your respect. Now, let me speak to her."*

I look up and hold out the receiver and the resignation in her eyes makes me hate her life.

She takes the phone and says smoothly, "Nonno."

I watch as she listens, a little of the fight leaving her, and then she stares at me with tears sparkling in her eyes and says softly, "I understand. Thank you."

She hands the phone back to me and I say, "Don Vieri."

His voice is laden with dark intent as he says huskily, *"My granddaughter is my heart, Mr. Romanov. Don't break it."*

He cuts the call, leaving me in no doubt of his intentions if anything happens to her and I sigh, replacing the phone and staring at her with concern.

"Are you okay?"

"I'm fine."

She takes a deep breath and fixes a smile on her face and says lightly.

"Now show me your room, Alexei, and make it a visit I won't ever forget."

CHAPTER 8

SERENA

*W*e head out of his office and once again, he takes my hand and I think back to our conversation earlier. I wasn't kidding. This really is the only way to travel, and I expect it's because of the man holding my hand so tenderly. He has surprised me. I expected him to be a player. It was obvious, but underneath that hard exterior is a gentle heart I wasn't expecting. It's almost as if he cares and that has surprised me.

He is the first man I have ever met who looks at me as if I count for something. He sees me as a woman first and who I am second. I like that and it causes my guard to drop and my heart to flutter because there is nothing else I wanted more.

It annoyed me, but I was touched that he was concerned for my family. Calling my grandfather was the right thing to do, and it surprised me. When nonno spoke to me, I feared the worst. He doesn't know I agreed to this before I knew the facts and just compromised my safety for a wild adventure. Alexei insinuated that it was done to protect me, which was probably the safest thing to do. However, we made a deal, and I am desperate to see it through and if anything, my grandfather's words made it even more desirable.

"I have every faith in you, princess. Alexei Romanov comes from a respectful family who we have dealt with on several occasions. I trust him with your life, and we will work together to discover any threats to your safety. Do not underestimate him, though. Remember who you are and what's at stake. Above all, be happy princess. That's all I want. I love you, so make this trip a short one and return home where you belong."

His message was clear. Be happy. Whatever that takes and right now it's being in the arms of the man who is fast becoming everything I wished for.

We head to his bedroom and as he pushes open the door, I take a deep breath, causing him to chuckle softly.

"Is the scent to your liking, little one?"

I step inside and nod slowly.

"Yes, this is what I've been looking forward to."

I gaze around his room and absorb every detail. The dark interior, the subdued lighting. Silk sheets and fur throws and plush carpeting. The mirrors set on all the walls increase its size and I catch our reflection and smile.

This is the moment it begins. Our wild adventure because I am in doubt at all its waiting for me in this room.

I turn and love how he changes before my eyes. Gone is the respectful host and in its place is a man who knows what he wants.

I stare into his eyes as I pull my hoody over my head, my t-shirt following and inch my leggings down with my thumbs and toss them to the side, standing before him in nothing but a black lacey bra and panties.

His eyes gleam as he does the same, revealing the hard cock of a man who knows what he wants.

He prowls the short distance and tugs me sharply against him and rips off my panties in one fluid movement.

I gasp as his thumb caresses my clit and his other one eases down the straps on my bra, his eager mouth finding my breast and sucking it in gently.

It feels so good, so delicious and then he drops to his knees and parting my thighs sucks my clit into his mouth, causing me to moan, "Fuck."

He pushes me until my legs hit the side of the bed and as I fall back, he devours me inside. So many sensations ripple through my body as he takes his fill and as my orgasm builds, he pulls away and growls, "Not yet."

He joins me on the bed and settles between my legs, his hard cock rubbing against my sodden pussy.

"So beautiful." He says, gazing into my eyes as his thumb rests against my lower lip and he presses it hard.

"Lie back and wait for me." His voice is husky and yet edged in dominance and as he leaves the bed, I feel my frustration mounting as I do as he says. The silk sheets are luxurious against my naked skin which causes me to stretch out with a soft sigh and when he returns, I stare at the silk scarves in his hands.

"Trust me tiger." He winks as he lifts my wrists and ties them together, pulling them over my head and hooking them to the bed post.

Then he places a blindfold around my eyes and whispers, "Prepare to be ruined."

My entire body is shaking as he drags a soft fur glove over my skin, which is so soft and decadent.

I'm aware that something cold enters me, causing me to cry out, and he says huskily, "It's only ice."

I hear a noise followed by a burst of hot air on my clit which causes me to pant as he whispers, "Hot and cold. How does that feel?"

"So good." I gasp as he rubs his thumb against my clit, causing the wet heat to trail from my body. He replaces his thumb with his mouth, and I shiver as he sucks and blows hot air on the rapidly melting ice and I hear a rustling as he says softly, "Condom. Are you ready for me, tiger?"

"God yeah."

I almost can't speak because so many sensations are consuming my body and I gasp as the blindfold is ripped from my eyes and he pulls my head up to face him and growls, "Watch me own your body."

He thrusts inside fast and hard, causing me to jerk back and as he grips my hair in one hand, he powers in, filling me completely. My pussy is drenched from melted ice and desire and, as he powers inside my body, he stares into my eyes the entire time. I have never known anything like this in my life. He was right. He *is* owning my body and I moan as he touches places I never knew existed, causing the mother of all orgasms to crash through me before I can prevent it. His own release isn't far behind and as he throbs inside me, wet tears roll from my eyes, which he kisses sweetly away.

"Did I hurt you, little one?" He says with a soft kiss to my lips, and I shake my head.

"No. It was, well, unexpected. Thank you."

He holds me close to his chest, and it is so good. As if he is protecting me from life and I could stay here forever.

We are high above the clouds soaring into unknown territory and, as adventures go, this one is everything I could have wished for.

He shifts to look at me and it's a little intense as he whispers, "Don't expect any sleep on this flight. Our time together is too precious for that."

My whole body vibrates at his statement because it reminds me this experience will be over soon and never repeated, and I'm not sure how I feel about that. On the one hand, it's what I wanted. A wild adventure and then to walk away with the memory.

"We should make it count." I say with a lustful gaze in his direction, and I love how his eyes burn with fierce heat as he towers over me, a willing sacrifice to his deviant mind.

CHAPTER 9

ALEXEI

I want to do unspeakable things to Serena Vieri, but I also want to make it count for something. As I stare into her soulful eyes, I see a woman who is struggling to deal with her birthright. She is hard, cool, and detached, but inside is a lost soul begging for freedom. I understand her life. She will be expected to play the loving granddaughter, marry for power, and take her place in her family business. I can already tell she is rebelling, and I understand a lot about that. My life is the same, but as a man I get to make my own choices up to a point. I chose freedom from marriage because marrying for power is not really an option when you have more of it than most.

Her heritage is inconvenient because now I feel responsible for her. Ruining her on this flight was the reason for my invitation, but that's now changed. I am protecting her and delivering her safely to her destination with her only threat coming from my voracious sexual appetite.

I'm surprised when she pushes me back and then turns so she sits astride me and as I stare into her eyes, I love the danger that flashes inside them as she says seductively, "Nothing has changed. I will use you for sex and you had better not hold out on me, Mr. Romanov. I expect great things from you. Don't let me down."

I have never seen a more glorious sight as she stares at me with a wicked expression of lust, disguising the yearning in her eyes and I reach up and roll my finger around her nipple and whisper, "Anything goes?"

She nods, licking her lips with a gaze of heated lust.

"Anything."

"That's a rash statement when you don't understand what that involves." I warn her and she shrugs.

"I have nothing to lose. We will be strangers soon and nobody will ever know. It stays here in the sky. We had a deal."

"Of course."

Reaching up, I run my hand around her neck and tug her sharply down to face me and as I draw that plump lower lip into my mouth, I suck it hard, causing her to groan.

I push inside her mouth and delight in locking her tongue with mine and taste a woman who is desperate for wicked abandon; a woman after my own heart.

She breaks free and whispers, "Now it's my time to give something back."

I say nothing as she presses soft kisses to my skin and moves further down my body, cupping my balls with a strong grip, causing me to groan.

Her fingernails dig into the soft skin and then her wicked mouth slides onto my cock, her tongue licking the tip and wrapping around it as she bites down softly.

"Fuck!" I love the sense of danger as she holds my balls in her fist and my cock against her teeth, knowing she is now controlling the whole of me. I can't think of anything else but the woman who is calling the shots and as I swell again inside her mouth, her low groan of appreciation makes me smile.

She slides my cock back and forth and I resist the urge to thrust in hard, right to the back, because I want to see where she's going with this. This is her show and I'm only the silent observer as she sucks my cock with a reverence that I love.

It's as if she is relishing every second, every movement and is in no hurry to get it over with. She is loving this; I can tell by the soft groans of appreciation that reach my ears as she delights in tasting me as I did her.

The pressure on my balls increases and it's so fucking hard not to thrust in deeper, but it's as if an angel is corrupting the devil and I don't want to break the spell she has over me.

She pulls out and heads further down my body, stopping at my feet with a wicked smile.

Then she fastens her gaze on mine as she gently sucks my toes, one by one, something that is strangely new to me. I like it. It's an erogenous zone I never knew I possessed, and as she massages the arch in my feet, she sucks my toes with obvious relish.

I have never been treated so reverently before. Usually, I am the one calling the shots and no woman has ever made it further than my cock. It appears that I end there, but not with Serena. She really does want the whole of me and I am happy to give it to her.

As she makes her way back up my body, I move fast and gripping her wrist hard, I flip her so she is face down on the bed and with one hand, I pull her ass high up in the air and growl, "My turn."

With one hand, I sheath my cock and then place one hand on either side of her hips and immediately enter her from behind. Thrusting forward roughly and without care, with the soul aim of marking her inside. She gasps as I push in fast, her head lunging forward at the force of it and as I fuck her hard, the dominant part of me roars because now she will discover what it's like to be owned by me.

I'm not soft, definitely not caring, and have an insatiable hunger to conquer and dominate. I unleash the cave man in me as I power in hard and fast, her strangled cries mixing with tortured groans as I unleash my inner wild beast and teach her who is really in charge.

I feel her sticky heat trailing around my rigid shaft and as I squeeze her swollen clit, I lean down and whisper, "Is this what you want, tiger? Am I wild enough for you?"

"It's not enough." She groans and, pulling back, I slap her hard on the ass, causing her to scream, "Oh, God!"

I thrust in harder this time, her head hitting the headboard as I ruin her body for my own pleasure. Once again, I press my thumb on her clit, causing her to tremble under me as she groans, "Harder."

I slap her ass hard and she screams as I grasp her hair and pull her head back as I use her body as if it is mine to ruin. I press down hard on her clit as I fill her completely and as she pants in my arms, I bite down sharply on her ear, causing her to scream, "Oh God, oh fucking God, as she comes apart under me. Her body throbbing, tensing and squeezing my cock as she milks every drop of cum from my balls as I shoot my load hard. It never seems to stop coming as I empty inside her, the condom trying hard to contain my load.

Our bodies are slick with sweat and satisfaction, but it's not enough. I am not done with her yet because time is against us. I must fit a lifetime of fucking this woman into a few short hours, so I pull her around to face me and kiss her long and hard, not caring that she has obviously lost the ability to hold herself up.

I tangle my fingers in her hair and love how it slides through my fingers and then I pull her up to her knees and cup her ass, inserting my finger into it causing her eyes to widen in shock as I growl, "Have you ever been fucked in the ass before?"

"No!" The horror in her eyes makes me grin and I whisper, "Then expect that answer to change by the end of this flight."

The way her eyes flicker with excitement makes me smile and once again, I kiss her hard, loving her ability to keep my interest.

As I come up for air, I whisper against her greedy lips, "I love the scent of you, Serena Vieri. Now I understand."

"What do I smell of?" She says with a wicked smile, and I say huskily, "You smell of my ownership."

"You arrogant jerk." She shakes her head in amusement and I nibble her ear and whisper, "You smell of sex, woman, and trouble."

"I'll take that." She laughs softly and I grip her face hard and stare into her eyes with a feral gleam in mine. "You don't smell nearly enough of me yet. I want you to reek of my scent. To turn heads as you pass, telling everyone who you belong to."

"I belong to no man." She hisses, her nails scratching my back as a warning and I grip her face harder and hiss, "You will never rid yourself of the scent of a Romanov because when you walk away from me, it will stay with you forever."

"If you say so." She rolls her eyes and then grips my balls hard, her nails digging in, which is surprisingly pleasant.

"What if I want you to smell of a Vieri, Alexei? When I walk away from you, it will linger in your sub conscious. You will remember it when you are fucking your next project and wish she was me."

She brushes her lips against my neck and then sucks the flesh in, marking my skin as I fully intend on marking hers and the combination of pleasure and pain is a heady cocktail as she squeezes my balls and bites my neck, her tits pressed against my chest as she fills my senses with her intoxicating scent.

Right now, Serena Vieri is owning me and not the other way around and what surprises me more than anything is how much I like it.

CHAPTER 10

SERENA

I love this. Lying beside Alexei with my head on his chest as he tangles his fingers in my hair, occasionally tugging it harder, reminding me I am dancing a fine line between pain and pleasure.

I trace a rose on his torso, loving the ink that decorates his muscled body, and I say reverently, "Your skin is a work of art. I love it."

"You have no ink on your skin?" He says with interest, and I press my lips to the rose and whisper, "No."

"Would you like some?"

I peer up at him and note the gleam in his eye and a shiver of excitement passes through me.

"What if I said yes?"

"Do you?"

"I said, what if?" I say with a roll of my eyes, and he grins.

"I can give you a rose anywhere you want."

"How?"

My heart starts racing as he lifts my chin up and stares at me with a dark expression that causes ripples of pleasure to flood through my body.

"I can tattoo your skin. It's a hobby of mine."

"What now?" I'm shocked and he nods as he sits up and pulls me up with him.

"I have the equipment and often give my staff tattoos to pass a long flight. I could decorate your skin and make it a memorable experience."

"You could?" I shake my head slowly. "How can I trust you not to make a mess of it?"

"You can't." He grins wickedly. "But you asked for a wild adventure and I'm offering you that."

"Okay then." My heart is racing as I agree to the most reckless thing I have ever done and that's saying something, considering where I am now.

"Where do you want it?" He says over his shoulder as he moves from the bed and heads over to a cupboard.

"Where nobody will see it, of course. I'm not that stupid."

He throws me a wicked grin and I can't help returning it. Then he says, "Lie back."

"You're doing it here. Are you crazy?" I say in shock, and he shrugs.

"Of course. I have everything I need here, and so you may as well be comfortable."

I am seriously wondering about my sanity as I lie naked on the stained sheets from the most irresponsible thing I've ever done and prepare for the next one.

There is no time to change my mind as he advances with a box that resembles one a beautician would carry.

I watch as he sets his equipment up and sits beside me, an alcoholic wipe in hand and then drags his hand across my body and says huskily, "Where will it be?"

"On my ass. You appear to be interested in that, so why not there?"

His low chuckle makes me smile, and he nods.

"Turn over and don't move."

I do as he says and bury my face in the soft pillow, wondering if I should be admitted to an asylum. It appears that control and madness go hand in hand and I'm not sure which one of us is crazier.

I feel the wipe against my skin and prepare to regret my impetuousness as something drags lightly against my ass.

"I'm drawing your tattoo, tiger."

"It had better *not* be a tiger, asshole." I growl and he leans down and whispers, "No. I'll be the one with the tiger tattoo by the end of this flight."

It shocks me because, for some reason, that has touched me more than anything. Would he really do that? Ink a tiger on his skin to remind him of this.

I fall silent as he works and only when the whine of the needle permeates the air do I suffer a moment of anxiety.

"Relax little one. I'll be gentle." He reassures me but I cry out as he begins and grip the sheets in my fist as he drags the needle against the soft skin of my ass.

"Relax." His hushed tones command me, and I try to think of anything else than what is happening now. I cry into the silk pillowcase, regretting my impetuousness and then, as the pain subsides, he drops a soft kiss on my ass, causing me to freeze immediately.

"Good girl." He whispers against my ear as his hand rubs a soft circle on my ass, dipping between it to caress my clit, causing me to gasp, "Is this part of your service?"

"Only with you." He chuckles against my ear as I feel his rigid cock nestling between my ass cheeks and he says huskily, "Pleasure and pain, that is what I can offer you and a lifetime reminder at the end of it."

"You had better be talking about the tattoo and not a baby." I groan, causing him to laugh and whisper, "If babies are conceived in your ass, that's a possibility."

"What the…" I jerk my head up and he forces it down and

whispers, "You'll love it."

His cock teases me from behind and I expect it's the whole forbidden scene we've got going on that makes me gasp, "Do it."

He lifts my ass with one hand under me and gently caresses my clit and says, "First the pain before the pleasure, followed by more pain."

He drops me and I hear the machine start up again and knowing what is coming after the pain is distinctly thrilling.

I can only concentrate on that as he resumes his work and after the initial pain, my body adjusts to it as he decorates my ass.

I'm not sure how much time passes before the machine stops and he lifts my ass up as before, his finger massaging my clit as he whispers, "Ready, tiger?"

"Okay." For some reason I am shy about this, which is a fucking joke considering what I'm letting him do and as his cock teases me from behind, I find myself waiting with disgusted anticipation for something that feels so wrong it can't be right.

He drags his cock through my wet heat that is betraying my dignity and, as he hovers at the entrance to my ass, he whispers, "This may be uncomfortable but go with it."

I don't say a word as he eases in gently, and he was right. It is uncomfortable and not particularly pleasant. Then he slides home, and I can't help the tortured moan that fills the air as he claims a part of me I didn't know was up for negotiation. It's so good as he moves in and out, filling me from behind, giving me an experience I never thought I'd have.

He plays with my clit and it scrambles my mind because this is the dirtiest thing I have ever done and I like it. He makes me wild in every way and as every emotion inside me battles to be the right one, I come so hard they all scatter for cover as he goes there, anyway.

He comes hard with a roar, and his hot cum fills my ass, dripping down my thighs, informing me I'm a disgusting whore. I am letting him desecrate my body in every way and I should be ashamed of myself.

I'm not.

I am liberated. As if I can take on the world and I expect it's because nobody will ever know how low I went but me. Alexei will walk away, and I will be happy to see him go, leaving me with the dirtiest secret to guard like I'm the only one who knows the whereabouts of the Holy Grail.

He pulls out and leaves me drowning in his semen as he continues his work on my ass, the pain no longer consuming my attention. All I feel is total relaxation. Multiple orgasms appear to conquer every other emotion and I lie wallowing in my own wantonness as I allow a stranger to tattoo my ass.

He could be writing anything, and I should be freaking out right now, but I'm not. All I'm thinking of is when we can do that again, which shows how far he has ruined me already. I know I won't walk out of here the same person who foolishly stumbled in, and I'll have a memento of that to live on me forever.

It's ages before he turns off the machine and presses something cold on my ass before pulling me up to a standing position.

"Come." He says with a wink and guides me across to the mirror and says proudly, "Turn around. It's a little red, but that will soon fade."

I peer anxiously into the mirror and stare at the small red rose that curls against my skin and, for some reason, it brings tears to my eyes.

He strokes my face and says with concern, "Don't you like it?"

"I…" I blink, the wet tears spilling down my face. "I love it, Alexei. Thank you."

I'm surprised to find that I do because he has created the most perfect delicate rose on my ass with jagged thorns protecting it.

We both admire his work, and he whispers, "I want to decorate your skin, little one. I want to create a masterpiece on top of nature's one. There are many images that come to mind that I want to see on you. It would be my finest work."

"You do?" I stare into his eyes as he cups my cheek and I lean into his rough hands, the ink covering them so sexy it makes my head spin.

He bends to kiss my lips and whispers, "Twenty-three hours is not enough time for what I have planned for you, Serena. I am regretting my terms and conditions already, but only have myself to blame."

I say nothing because I feel it too. The more time I spend with him, the more I fear the clock ticking. I never want to wake up from this dream because I have everything I want flying high above the clouds.

Freedom, abandonment from my responsibilities, and him. The man who makes me believe I can conquer the world. The man who has made me fearless and yet fearful at the same time.

What the fuck have I done?

CHAPTER 11

ALEXEI

When I inked the rose on Serena's ass, I loved every minute of it. Knowing I was marking her virgin ass forever was a serious turn on. Picturing what I would inevitably do made the experience almost a religious one, and when I finally claimed her virgin territory, I felt like a conquering hero.

Now she will wear my mark forever and there will be no escaping the memory every time she looks in the mirror. I am incredibly proud of what I have done and only hope she doesn't regret it when she walks away.

Being here in this room, naked and free, is a flight I won't forget in a hurry. I have entertained many women here before. Not in this room, but in the one Serena dismissed out of hand.

Now I'm glad she did because I am also experiencing new horizons and she is the perfect person to share that with.

I say with a wicked grin, "We should get some food. Watch a movie, perhaps?"

"Why?" She looks confused. "We just ate."

"Because I have another adventure in mind."

"What is it?" The sparkle in her eyes makes me chuckle and I toss her a robe and say evenly, "You can't shower for twenty-four hours. I will dress your tattoo with a bandage."

"You mean I can't clean up?" Her eyes widen. "I reek of sex."

"Good." I raise my eyes. "I thought you loved my scent."

"I do." She laughs out loud, and I stare at the beauty who happened into my life.

"Okay. Do what you must and prove to me I was right to accept your offer."

I bandage her ass with a medicated dressing and after we pull on our robes, we head out of the door, hand in hand.

As we walk, she says nervously, "I hope we don't see anyone. They will think I'm a whore."

I shrug. "They won't think anything."

"Because they are used to this, I suppose." She sounds a little sad and I stop and grip her face in my hand and say harshly, "I never hold a woman's hand. I never entertain them in my room, and I never devote my entire flight to them. You are special, Serena because you are the first person I've wanted to treat this way. Nobody will think badly of you. They will know of my respect for you and understand you are worth more to me than a quick fuck to pass the time on a flight."

Her eyes fill with grateful tears, and she whispers, "Well, you're just a fuck to me."

It makes me laugh out loud and as I kiss her words away, I pull back and say gruffly, "I'm glad to hear it."

* * *

WE HEAD to the theater and I can tell Serena is glad of the darkness and we settle on a couch at the back. Several other ones are already occupied as my staff relax on the long flight.

Serena whispers, "Are you freaking kidding me?"

"What?" I say with amusement, already knowing the object of her distaste.

"You brought me here to watch a fucking porno?"

Loud moans fill the theater as the actors enjoy an orgy on the screen and I laugh softly. "I never chose this. Blame my staff." I shrug. "They're men, Serena. Why wouldn't they choose a porno?"

"What, they don't like James frigging Bond or something. This is disgusting."

Her eyes are wide as she stares at the naked bodies on the screen as one woman is impaled from both sides.

Serena's robe is open enough to glimpse a view of her breast and I reach inside and caress her nipple as she stares at the screen.

She says nothing, which makes me smile as she regards the scene with a morbid curiosity and as I move lower, my fingers find her clit, rubbing it gently as her legs part naturally. She still doesn't even look in my direction as I insert two fingers inside her as the actors moans and cries fills the theater and as I pump hard, her eyes roll back and she gasps as I massage her clit and thrust inside, her sticky heat coating my fingers.

Nobody can see us. We are under the cover of darkness, which adds to the drama and her soft pant tells me she is so turned on by this as I bring her to an orgasm that I catch in my hand.

I lick my fingers one by one, her heated gaze turning to face me, and she moves her hand to grip my hard cock.

This time I settle back as she pumps it hard, caressing my balls as the actors fuck on the screen and as I'm about to cum, she dips her head in my lap and takes my cock into her mouth and sucks every drop of cum that spurts from my body.

Her tongue cleans up and as she sits, she smiles at me with a wicked gleam in her eyes as she leans back and watches the movie with a satisfied smile on her face.

We sit in silence and after a few minutes, I notice her hand moving inside her robe as she pleasures herself, glancing at me with a wicked smile on her face as her hands move effortlessly over her body. I am so turned on I can't look away as she shows me what she likes.

I have never seen such an alluring sight in my life, and I can't tear my eyes away from her and I watch as she orgasms under her own hand, staring into my eyes the entire time as the noise of a fucking orgy emanates from the screen.

When she finishes, she leans toward me and whispers, "This beats anything the airline had planned."

It makes me laugh and I drag her lips to mine, needing the contact because right in this moment it strikes me that I have met my match in every way and if she thinks she's walking away from me when we land, she's about to learn a hard lesson.

* * *

THE MOVIE FINISHES and as the next one begins, I take her hand and lead her from the theater toward the rear of the aircraft.

"Where are we going?" She says with interest, and I say with a smile. "To eat."

"The restaurant?"

"No. I have a private dining room for when I require privacy."

"Of course you do." She rolls her eyes and walks beside me, holding my hand as if we are a normal couple.

As we walk, Gleb appears from a doorway and says with a sigh, "Could you spare me a minute, Alexei?"

I peer at him sharply because it's obvious this can't wait and so I nod. "Give me five minutes."

He retreats into his office and as we walk, Serena says with concern, "He didn't appear happy."

"He never looks happy." I reply with a roll of my eyes, and she shakes her head. "I suppose it comes with the territory. I'm guessing you are a demanding boss."

"Of course. I'm demanding in every aspect of my life. Haven't you figured that out yet?"

"It's a quality I admire."

I grin as I push the door open and show her into the private dining room that has a larger window than most in the plane and offers a stunning view of the sun going down.

"Wow! This is amazing." She gasps and despite my promise to Gleb, I say darkly, "Take off your robe."

She doesn't even question me and drops it to the floor, and I stare in wonder at the scene before me. She looks like a goddess as she stands before the disappearing sun, the glorious vista of red and orange mixing with the darkness behind her.

I say nothing and openly stare as she watches me with shining eyes and I say with regret, "Thank you."

"What for?"

"For the image that will be forever imprinted on my memory. You are beautiful. A tiger who is more majestic than the sun that bows down before her."

"So, you're a poet now?" She fastens her robe and grins.

"I am everything, little one. I'm surprised you haven't realized that yet."

I point to the table that has been set for two and say with a regretful sigh.

"Make your choices and order them for us both. I shouldn't be long."

"You trust my choices, after I recklessly agreed to come here with you?"

She shakes her head. "I'll try to make it memorable."

"It already is tiger."

I wink as I leave her to a rare moment alone, hoping like fuck Gleb has a good reason to pull me away from her side.

CHAPTER 12

SERENA

I'm not sure why but it's as if a part of me is now missing. As soon as he closed the door, I felt the loss. What's happening to me? Why am I bothered about him leaving? He will soon enough, so I had better get used to it.

I fasten the robe tightly and take a seat at the table, staring at the view with a sense of calm that is surprising. I'm never calm and always looking out for problems. Waiting for the next order issued from my family, who think they have the right to govern my life.

This was a spontaneous act of rebellion against that, and I still can't believe I pulled it off.

The door opens, making me jump and I watch a woman enter dressed in the same uniform the attendant who greeted us wore.

"Good evening, Miss Vieri."

She says respectfully and her smile could light up a room. She's a pretty girl, and it unsettles me a little. I'm guessing Alexei surrounds himself with pretty women and it shouldn't matter because I am on a temporary visa here, anyway.

I return her smile as she hands me a menu and says respectfully, "Can I fetch you a drink from the bar?"

"Water will be fine. Actually, second thoughts, I could murder an espresso."

She nods. "Of course."

As she turns to leave, I say with interest. "Excuse me."

She turns and I feel a little foolish as I say, "I was just wondering about your job. I mean, is there a large crew onboard?"

She nods. "There are ten of us, including the flight crew. We work for the Romanov family and as they travel a lot, we are kept busy.

"So, Alexei shares this plane with his family."

I feel silly asking, and she nods with a small smile. "Yes."

"Are there many members of the Romanov family?"

I don't know why I'm asking, really, but she doesn't appear to think this conversation strange and just nods.

"Yes. Mr. Romanov senior and his wife, his four sons, one of which is Alexei and their sister. There are also two uncles and their sons and daughters. They are quite the dynasty."

I am interested in hearing about them and as she turns to leave, I say quickly, "Do they all work together in the same company?"

"Of course. They run the family businesses together and every member has a seat on the board. I'm surprised you haven't heard of them."

She smiles and says gently, "Anyway, I should fetch that coffee. Shall I bring Mr. Romanov his usual?"

"Yes. Um, thank you."

She leaves and I feel a little foolish at having to ask her at all. It only reinforces the fact I'm a stranger who couldn't resist her devastatingly attractive boss. It wouldn't surprise me if she has entertained him herself, then I feel bad for thinking the worst of her. She was so sweet and kind and probably has a boyfriend at home and this is pure business.

I consider what she told me and I kind of know a lot about family businesses.

As I stare around at the opulence surrounding me, it only demonstrates how successful they are. We are no strangers to owning a private jet, but this is something else. It makes the Vieris look like paupers, and it intrigues me.

The attendant soon returns and sets down a jug of water and the desired espresso, alongside a glass of clear liquid for Alexei.

She notes my interest and grins. "Vodka. He is Russian after all."

It makes me laugh. "He certainly is."

As I stare at the menu, I can't concentrate because so many things are running through my mind right now and the fact she is waiting patiently heaps the pressure on a little and I say with a sigh, "Just tell the chef to surprise us. It would be a lot easier."

"Good choice, madam."

She takes the menu and I say quickly, "Do you work all the time, or do you get days off with your family?"

I realize I'm prying into her personal life, but this whole set up intrigues me.

She doesn't seem to care, though. "I have rostered days off and am part of three crews who alternate. We mainly work for Alexei but occasionally crew for other members of the family when the hours don't work out."

"It sounds an interesting job. You must have seen some amazing places."

I kind of envy her because she enjoys seeing the world in luxurious surroundings.

"I love my job," she positively beams. "But home is Moscow."

I stare at her in surprise. "You don't sound Russian."

There is not a trace of an accent in her voice and if anything, I would say she's American.

"I married a Russian." She winks. "We met on board. He is one of the pilots."

"So, you travel together. That's amazing."

She nods. "It is."

I don't know why that makes me so happy and I'm guessing it's because it removes her from Alexei's bed, and I hate how shallow I am. He doesn't owe me anything at all and it's no concern of mine who he sleeps with.

She leaves me alone and I lean back in my seat and picture life after Alexei Romanov. For some reason, I can't picture it at all and I realize I am getting in too deep, despite my terms and conditions at the beginning.

As I stare out at the darkness, I feel at home. Yes, darkness is my friend because it's never been any different and probably never will. If someone is out to kill me, I wish they would get on with it because waiting for it to happen is like living in hell.

CHAPTER 13

ALEXEI

The minute I open the door, I know something bad has happened from the grave expression in Gleb's eye and the two glasses of vodka waiting on the desk. He is sitting in the one opposite my usual chair and he stands respectfully as I cross the room to take my seat.

"Tell me." I say roughly because there is no point in wasting words.

"I am sorry to be the bearer of sad news, Alexei."

Gleb's face is set in stone and my heart is thumping so hard he can probably hear it.

I stare at him with a hard expression, and he says reverently, "I'm sorry to inform you that your father passed away suddenly this afternoon."

I say nothing and stare at him in shock as I struggle to process his words.

The seconds drag like hours as I try to understand what this means and then I nod to the glass on the desk and we take one each and hold them high, whispering, "May his soul rest in peace."

I drain the glass, but it does fuck all to help with the pain I'm feeling right now. I sit down heavily as Gleb refills the glass and I shake my head.

"How did he die?"

"I believe it was natural causes."

Gleb says kindly. "A heart attack that came on suddenly. Your mother reported he was unwell after dinner, and he retired to his bed. It was quick, so I understand."

It's as if I am hollow inside. I have no emotion at all, just an emptiness I can't deal with right now.

I drag my fingers through my hair and drain the second glass, but it may as well be water for all the effect it has.

There is a deep pain inside me as I come to terms with the fact I will never see him again and I feel so alone.

My father is dead.

I have never known pain like this.

Gleb drags my attention back with practical common sense and says firmly, "Your presence has been requested at your family home. Shall I instruct the pilot to change course for Russia?"

"Of course." My voice sounds dull, as if it doesn't even belong to me, and the tears burn brightly behind my eyes as I face life without the formidable head of the Romanov family at the helm.

"Miss Vieri, shall I arrange a connecting flight to Sydney for her?"

Gleb says practically, his words strangely shocking me to shout, "Fuck no! She comes with me."

If he's surprised, he doesn't show it and just nods. "Then I will arrange for a message to be delivered to her family."

Fuck!

I make a fist and thump the desk, hating the fact I'm falling apart. I can't think of anything other than my grief right now, but there is no way in hell I'm letting Serena out there unprotected with an assassin in the shadows.

"How long?" I say with a ragged breath, and he says coolly, "We have two hours remaining of flight time."

"Make the arrangements."

I stand and leave, not caring about anything but getting away from this room. My father is dead, and I never even got to say goodbye. Why would I? He wasn't ill, at least he never let on, which makes it even worse somehow.

I HEAD to my bedroom and slam the door behind me, sinking to the floor with my back to the wall. I am alight with grief and there is a gaping hole inside me that my father used to fill and if anything, it is leaking emotion that will be difficult to replace.

I must sit for only minutes, but it seems like hours before I drag myself up and reach for my cell phone.

I'm surprised when she answers immediately.

"Alexei." Her soft voice sounds broken, which doesn't help, and I whisper softly, "I'm sorry, mama."

"I know."

Just hearing her gentle voice gives me a yearning to be with her and I hate that it will take over two hours until I am by her side.

"It was so sudden. One minute he was complaining about the food and the next he was dead."

Her tearful voice tears me apart as she sobs, *"It happened so quickly, we didn't have time to react. The doctor was called immediately, but he was dead before he arrived."*

Her sobs drive the pain deep into my heart as she whispers, *"Hurry home, my son. I need you."*

She cuts the call and I note several texts lit up on my phone, mainly from my brothers in the group chat and as I read them, I hate that I'm so far away.

We are always scrambled across the globe dealing with shit and rarely together unless for family occasions. This is our life. None of us are married with families of our own and I hate that my father never got to be a grandfather. He will never see his son's children, not that I intend on having any, but it's at times like this it becomes important.

I type out my own reaction and hate how cold it looks.

> I'll be there as soon as this god-damned plane lands.

Luckily, my sister Anastasia is already with mama, so at least she's not on her own. As always, we'll gather around her and ensure she has everything she requires. She won't be left alone, and my heart aches for her.

Theirs was a true love story. The American heiress who fell in love with a traveling businessman. Despite her parents' anger at their marriage, they made it happen and my father had the last laugh. He became richer and more powerful than her parents and they came to him for help when the stock market crashed, and they lost everything.

Karma's a bitch, and we have always been taught to value money. To work hard and never stop hustling because you never know when it may end.

I stare around my room and the dark, depressing walls are closing in on me. The only person I need right now is the alluring body and compelling eyes of my goddess. I want to lose myself in her delicious flesh, hear her soft voice moan my name, and I want her to make me forget. I need her more than I have ever needed anyone before, and so I head off in search of oblivion.

CHAPTER 14

SERENA

*I*t's been ages since Alexei left and I'm beginning to get worried, but then the door crashes open and he heads into the room with a face like thunder, turning the lock to trap us inside. I stare at him in shock as his eyes flash and he walks toward me with the air of a lion about to strike.

I should be very afraid right now but there is something bad happening and I jump up and say fearfully, "What is it?"

"No words." He says in a husky voice, and I watch as he sweeps the contents of the table to the floor, the noise of breaking glass shocking me into submission.

He pulls me roughly toward him and tears off my robe, so I am trembling before him and then he shocks me by pulling me hard against his chest, his arms wrapping around my body and holding me so tightly I almost can't breathe. He buries his face in my hair and inhales sharply, and I can already tell he is falling apart.

I say nothing at all and let him deal with whatever has happened and as his breathing comes under control, he drags my head back by my hair and kisses me with a deep sense of urgency that shocks me. He fists my hair and grips it tightly, holding my head in place as he devours me.

Then he pushes me back on the table and spreads my legs with his hands and nestles his head between my thighs, taking a leisurely swipe against my clit, which causes me to groan out loud.

He says nothing and I'm not about to as he moves up my body before dropping his pants and burying himself deep inside me.

"Fuck, Alexei." I squeal as the shock hits me.

"You're not wearing a fucking condom."

He pulls back, still buried deep inside me, and there is a strange, crazed look in his eye as he growls, "Perhaps I don't want protection. Maybe I want a fucking kid with you."

"Excuse me." I stare at him in shock as he grins, a wicked expression that has zero emotion attached to it.

He moves slowly and steadily inside me, stretching every limit I possess, and it feels so damn good I'm not complaining anymore. He stares at me the entire time with the aura of a predator and it's so incredibly sexy I lose my mind as well as my dignity as he fucks me hard.

My back scrapes against the table as he thrusts in hard, and from the desolation in his eyes, he's not in control of his actions.

I should stop him, push him away, but I love it. I love the fact he is laid bare before me. His pain written all over his face as he stares at me with a lost expression. It draws me in and makes me want to tear down continents to find who has hurt him and so I stare into his eyes with a promise as he fucks me hard, not breaking eye contact at all.

I am sore, bruised inside and I'm burning up, but he doesn't stop fucking me as if it's the only thing he can do. It's quite unnerving but sexy at the same time because right at this moment, it's only the two of us in his world. He is gazing at me with an intensity that shocks me, and yet I love it. I reach up and drag my fingers through his hair and tug it hard, forcing a reaction from the man who is focused solely on me.

"I want to fuck new life into you, tiger." He growls. "A life for a life. A son. I want a son."

"Fuck, Alexei, what are you saying?"

He grips my face hard between his hands and growls, "There is only one woman up to the job, and I'm inside her now. Tell me you're not on birth control."

I should be afraid of the manic expression in his eye, but I love it. It's possessive, animalistic and so damn sexy I'm a mess inside. I have never felt so needed in my life and if a child comes into the world because of this moment, it will be a special one because sadly I am on birth control, but he really doesn't need to know that right now.

I lower my eyes because I can't do it. I can't lie to him, but I don't want to disappoint him either. I want to be his everything because a man has never looked at me as if I am. The way he is gazing at me now is so powerful I would agree to anything he asked just for this attention again.

With a rough curse, he comes so hard I feel his cock throbbing inside me as he spills his seed deep into my womb. He pushes in deeper and roars like a lion, and the raw pain in that sound brings tears to my eyes.

He pulls out suddenly and surprises me by dragging me to the floor with him, wrapping his arms around me from behind, cradling me like a baby, and burying his face in my hair.

His cum is dripping from inside me and I bear the scars of his torment inside. My pussy is throbbing and sore and my back is painful from scraping against the table. I should feel used, abused even, but I don't. I feel loved and for a woman who doesn't really know what that is like, it's the best thing in the world.

* * *

TIME PASSES and we sit on the floor, the wreckage of the table surrounding us. There are no words and no communication other than soft touches and intermittent kisses as he struggles to deal with whatever has happened.

Then he sighs heavily and brushes his lips against my neck and whispers, "Forgive me, little one. I lost control, and you were the recipient of that."

His words shock me because it's as if it would have happened whoever stood before him, and I hate that I don't feel special anymore. It makes the tears collect behind my eyes and I blink them furiously away, determined he will never see how much his words have hurt me.

He stands and says with a sigh, "Come, we should clean up. We will be landing soon."

"So soon." I'm shocked and he nods, wrapping my robe around me in a sweet show of chivalry before tying the belt in a double knot.

"We must make a detour."

"Where?" My heart is beating so fast as he says in a dead voice, "Russia. I am needed at home."

"What happened?" I am afraid but not for me—for him and he says in a gruff voice, "My father is dead."

Then he unlocks the door and heads outside without another glance in my direction.

CHAPTER 15

ALEXEI

I am out of control. I *never* lose control. What just happened was a reaction that shocked me. I didn't consider Serena at all as I fucked my grief into her, blurting out I wanted a child with her—a son. Where the fuck did that come from? I can't deal with the shit that's happening to me, but more importantly, I can't let her go either.

When Gleb told me he would arrange a connecting flight for her, it made me panic. It was as if I was losing her too, and it sent me over the edge. She stays with me, but fuck knows why. I don't need women. I don't need her—not really. Then why is it so good when I am buried deep inside her?

At that moment, I was home. In a place I belonged where I felt safe. She provided a sanctuary, and I never wanted to leave. It's why I overstayed my welcome and she must be suffering from the effects of that.

I can't even offer her a deep bath to cleanse the burn because of that fucking tattoo. I am officially out of control and yet the one thing I'm sure of is I don't want to let her out of my sight.

* * *

WE HEAD BACK to my bedroom, and I hate the tension that is building between us and so I lock the door and lean against it, and say huskily, "I'm sorry, little one. You didn't deserve that."

"Deserve what?' She appears angry and I don't blame her.

"The way I was back there. I lost control and I apologize."

"It's fine." She turns away and I can tell she is upset and it's probably because of how I just treated her.

"Come." I nod toward the bathroom.

"You can't get the tattoo wet, so allow me to help."

"I don't need your help." She bites back and I sigh heavily. "You may not *need* my help, but you're fucking getting it whether you agree or not."

She swivels around slowly and stares at me with fury flashing in her eyes.

"You arrogant bastard. How dare you speak to me like that!"

It makes me laugh because right in this moment she has never looked so beautiful to me and as I cross the room, she makes a dive for her gun that is exactly where we left it what seems like a lifetime ago.

I reach it first and kick it under the bed and, gripping her wrists, I restrain her with her back to me. She attempts to get away but I'm too good at this and whisper, "I'm sorry, tiger. If you'll let me explain, I'll apologize properly."

"Okay, but it will take a lot for me to forgive you, Alexei."

My heart sinks because she is probably angry at how I treated her.

"Come. We'll talk in there."

I lead her to the bathroom and run the shower, gently easing the robe from her shoulders, strangely proud of the marks I left on her body. I was rough, and the bruising is coming out and as I spin her around, I pull her flush against me.

"Please forgive me. It's not every day your father dies, and I reacted badly. I didn't mean to treat you like that, but all I wanted was to be inside you."

"Why?" She stares at me with compassion, and I stroke her face lightly and lean my head against hers, whispering, "I don't deal with emotion well. There is something about you, Serena Vieri, that draws me to you. Like a magnetic force that I couldn't resist if I tried. When I heard the news, my first thought was about my mother and then you. I needed you for some reason, and that scares the hell out of me. I don't need anyone, but I did need you. I *do* need you."

Her eyes are wide and filled with emotion as she strokes my face and whispers, "Thank you. I thought..." She breaks off and shakes her head. "It doesn't matter, but thank you for clearing that up, at least."

She smiles softly, and it makes me happy, and I lead her half in the shower and place some soap on a flannel and proceed to wash her by hand.

"My father was a good man." I start to open up to her, which again surprises me because I never talk about family—ever.

"No, scrub that. He was a great man who made billions by clever decisions and a lot of luck along the way. He was ruthless but fair and we were brought up to respect others and yet distance ourselves from emotion. Business was the only thing that mattered, and it always came first."

My mind wanders back to my childhood, and I smile at the happy memories.

"We were a tight family. Close in age and there were five of us."

"Your poor mom." She laughs softly and I nod.

"It must have been hard, but she never complained. We were a happy family, we always have been, but we were brought up to be tough where it counted."

I continue to care for her, loving the intimacy between us, and say softly, "My father had many enemies. He was too ruthless not to, and we soon learned to protect ourselves. Mikhail, my younger brother, excels at intimidation and took over the security aspect of our business. I'm sure you understand what that job involves."

She nods. "Perfectly."

I shrug. "He is also on his way back from Australia, so Regina has escaped death this time."

I add with a hard glint in my eye. "For now, anyway."

I rub shampoo through her hair and massage it in carefully and say with a hard edge to my voice.

"So, I need to keep you close. I will not send you to your destination without protection. That is why you must accompany me to my family's home, and I apologize in advance for that."

"I see."

If anything, her face drops and I am compelled to say, "I can't let you walk away from me, Serena because as it turns out, twenty-three hours is a drop in the ocean to the time I want to spend with you."

She looks up and stares at me with an expression I can't place and then she whispers, "Thank you for telling me that, Alexei. It means a lot. More than you know."

I merely smile and carry on cleaning her up, my mind wandering back home, wondering if I'll be able to cope with what will happen there.

CHAPTER 16

SERENA

*A*lexei has withdrawn again and as we dress back in our traveling clothes, we do it in silence.

He is preoccupied and I know better than to attempt conversation. He is grieving and I suppose I would be the same and all I can do is to be here for him as he was for me. It touched me when he said he wanted to protect me. He doesn't owe me that.

I'm still convinced I wasn't the intended target, but that all seems like a lifetime ago now.

All that matters is getting him through the ordeal that is sure to be waiting for him and I can't deny that I am interested in seeing his life first-hand. The Romanov dynasty. Why do I like the sound of that so much?

Our wild adventure has turned a corner and is heading in a different direction, and I'm not sure how I feel about that. I was kind of counting on twenty-three hours of reckless behavior before normal life resumed.

Now it's a continuation of that, but in a very different place. I have never been to Russia before and it kind of scares me. I don't know why because I'm not one prone to fear anything. I suppose it's the unknown, but at least I will have Alexei watching over me.

We make our way to the bar that is set in the front of the aircraft, and I stare with curiosity at the people surrounding us. They seem familiar to me. Men with many tattoos and fuck off attitudes. There are a few in suits who are working on laptops and a couple of women who are checking their phones.

Nobody gives us a second look and I like that. I usually live my life in a goldfish bowl, the subject of interest everywhere I go. If I'm at home, it's as if I'm being scrutinized and in public it's no different, largely due to the number of guards surrounding me.

I like this anonymity and as we sit at a table, Alexei heads to the bar and I study him with growing interest. He doesn't expect to be served like my family does. He is engaged in conversation with the man beside him, who appears at ease with him. When he returns, he is carrying two espressos, which makes me smile.

"Is something funny, little one?" He sets them down on the table and I shrug. "We're in a bar. I expected you to return with your usual vodka."

"I need to keep a clear head." He sighs as he sits opposite me and leans back in his seat. "This won't be a fun visit, Serena. My family doesn't deal with emotion well and will be worse than normal."

"In what way?"

He shrugs. "They will fight their grief and deal with it badly. I think you've been on the receiving end of that."

I shake my head and smile sadly. "Any emotion is welcome, Alexei. I know a lot about hiding it and my family is the same. We give an outward appearance of cool detachment, but inside is a struggle to keep any feelings away. It's the mafia way and obviously the Romanov way, too. Don't worry about me, I get it."

To my surprise, he reaches across the table and takes my hand and squeezes it gently, staring into my eyes with a grateful expression.

"Thanks for understanding, little one. It means a lot."

I have no words because moments like this are rare in my life. I have never been treated like this. As an equal. Somebody of importance and I like it. My family does, to an extent, but I always feel as if I'm tolerated. As long as I play my part, they approve. The fact I ditched my protection and ran off with a stranger won't have gone down well, but Alexei has diffused that particular bomb and they will never know.

I watch him closely and it appears he has withdrawn into himself as he gazes out of the window, his hand resting on mine across the table. I say nothing and just direct furtive glances his way, not really understanding what is going on between us.

As soon as the seatbelt signs illuminate, we strap ourselves in and with a deep sense of regret, the dream is over.

* * *

I'M USED to traveling in convoy, but this is something else.

Lines of black cars are waiting for us and as we disembark the aircraft, the passengers fill them. The luggage is loaded onto a truck at the back and there is a guard on every door that I recognize. Dressed in black with black shades, obviously armed, both with a gun and a don't fuck with me attitude.

Alexei directs me to one in the middle and as we take our seats, the guard nods respectfully and closes the door. As we set off, Alexei stares out of the window, not even attempting to make conversation, but I understand why. I would feel the same if I was in his position and so I gaze out of the window at the passing scenery with interest.

I am pleasantly surprised. I always imagined Russia as cold and filled with snow. This place is sunny with blue skies, the trees are green, and the landscape is impressive. I am fascinated by it and act like an eager tourist as I stare at a place I never imagined visiting.

The time passes so quickly I'm astonished when the cars slow down and Alexei sighs. "This is home, little one. I'm sorry to put you through this ordeal."

I stare out at the huge, majestic gates that keep everyone out while the security guards check every car inside. It takes a while because there are so many and as we reach our turn, I'm intrigued when Alexei rolls down the window and the guard says something in Russian and then nods respectfully.

Alexei nods and the guard steps back and waves us through and as the window closes, I say with curiosity, "Why is security so tight?"

"Because Russia is a dangerous place, little one. My family has many enemies and leave nothing to chance."

"I see." It's no different with my family, but I thought it would be for the Romanovs. They are businessmen first, not mafia. Perhaps I got that wrong.

The drive to the house takes a further ten minutes and I gaze out on parkland and landscaped gardens as we pass. This is wealth on a grand scale, and I should have known really from by the size of their plane.

Most of the other cars head somewhere else but the car in front of ours and the one behind stop outside a huge front entrance and as we come to a stop, I stare out at a mansion that would rival a large country hotel. White marble gleams in the sunlight and there appears to be nothing out of place. It's the grandest house I have ever seen, and I blink as the huge front door opens and a uniformed servant stands to attention.

The car door opens, and I wouldn't be surprised to see his fucking black carpet rolled out for us to walk on because it's as if royalty has come to town.

Alexei offers me his hand and as we step out, he squeezes it gently before pulling me along with him inside the mansion.

Once again, the servant says something respectfully in Russian, and Alexei nods but says nothing in return.

As we head inside, I'm surprised to see two women waiting for us and Alexei turns to me and says with an apology in his eyes.

"You must go with Maria and Alina, and they will show you to your rooms. I must go to my mother. I'll come and find you when I have dealt with my family."

"Of course." I hate that he is walking away from me, but completely understand why. This is not the time for visitors. That is obvious from the solemn faces of the staff and the black and white flowers that have replaced more joyful ones. This is a family in mourning and the evidence is everywhere.

"Miss. Vieri." One of the women steps forward. "I am Alina, and my colleague is Maria. We will be honored to assist you during your stay."

"Thank you." I smile as Maria nods and moves off, and Alina waves for me to follow her.

There is no conversation as we walk through a majestic entrance and down a long corridor that appears to be carved from marble. Discreet lighting illuminates our way, and we reach an archway at the end that leads to a huge door. As we head through it, I realize we have left the main house and are heading toward what appears to be another one set in the grounds.

Alina explains, "This is the guest house. One of many on the property. You will find everything you need here."

"It's beautiful." I stare in awe at the miniature version of the main house, although it could certainly accommodate a large family. It has its own grounds and appears to be completely self-contained, and I'm very relieved about that.

I am overwhelmed and as we head inside, I gaze around in awe at the splendor before me. Marble floors and textured walls lead up to a painted ceiling that any great artist would be proud to call their own work. There are portraits on the walls of formidable looking men and women and the huge sweeping staircase set in the center rises majestically upward to a galleried landing.

Maria heads up there and as we follow, I try desperately to take it all in and Alina says softly, "This house is yours for your stay. Maria and I will be your staff and anything you need, night or day, will be our pleasure to provide."

I can't even speak because I am blown away by their hospitality and am beginning to believe my own family are paupers in comparison to the Romanovs. First the plane and now this. I thought we had it all, apparently not.

The women show me to a suite of rooms I'm almost positive royalty would be impressed by and as I stare around at the pretty rooms, I'm impressed.

I feel extremely scruffy in my leggings and hoody. I haven't even packed any suitable evening wear because when I visit mom, it's on a ranch in the middle of nowhere and formal attire is not required. I am well out of my comfort zone and feel like a fraud and as the women fuss around me, showing me around and pointing out everything I should know, I am drowning in imposter syndrome.

CHAPTER 17

ALEXEI

I waste no time in locating my mother and as I walk into the formal reception room, my heart breaks when I regard her frail figure dressed in black, sitting by the window overlooking the garden. Anastasia sits with her and stands as I enter.

"Alexei." Her eyes brim with tears as she heads to my side and I wrap her in my arms and whisper, "It's good to see you, Ana."

She clings on tightly and then pulls back, and we both head toward to our mother.

Her grief-stricken face stares up at me and I drop to my knees before her and pull her into my arms.

"I'm sorry mama." I kiss her soft cheek as she weeps in my arms and the pain is almost unbearable as we grieve together. Ana wipes the tears from her eyes as we say nothing at all, and mama's gentle sobs are the only sound in the room.

After a while, she pushes me away and says with a brave sad smile, "I am so lost without him."

"We all are." Ana says with a sniff, and I sigh heavily. "Where is he?"

"In the church. We will head there now."

I take her arm and with my sister on her other side, we begin the short walk to the family chapel set in the grounds. It's a beautiful day and as we walk through the gardens, mama says sadly, "Andrei loved this time of year. He always said the house was at its finest."

We say nothing as she continues. "It will seem so empty without him."

It concerns me because mama will be alone here when we all leave, and a widow's existence is very different to one as a powerful man's wife. She will be left alone to grieve and disregarded from society. She is of no further use because the man she accompanied is no longer around. It concerns me because mama is a beautiful woman, only just sixty years of age and could live a great number of years in isolation. She has no grandkids, no daughters-in-law to occupy her time and she will find living as a widow extremely difficult.

Anastasia works as a lawyer in her own company, taking care of the Romanov family business interests and is always incredibly busy. She will have no time to devote to her mother because business always comes first to a family that considers it its top priority.

"I understand you brought someone with you, son. A girl."

Mama's voice sounds a little lighter and loaded with curiosity, and I nod. "She is business. Nothing more."

Ana shakes her head as mama says sadly, "Oh, I, well, never mind."

The look Ana directs my way makes me feel like an asshole, especially because I consider Serena far more than just business, so I sigh heavily and say impatiently, "I like her. That's all you need to know."

Mama smiles even though she tries to disguise it and Ana nods her appreciation. Anything that brings a smile to mama's face is worth its weight in gold and if I can give her a little pleasure and some hope while I'm here, I'll be happy to oblige.

We head into the church and the mood darkens as soon as I see the casket laid on a stand before the altar. Mama starts to weep and brushes the ever-present tears away with the back of her hand.

She steps forward and takes my hand and whispers, "Go to your father and pay your last respects."

I kiss her cheek and hate how heavy my heart is inside me and as my feet drag me to the coffin, I steel myself to look inside.

When I see my father lying there, defeated in death, the pain is immeasurable. He could be sleeping. He looks so peaceful, and I wonder what ran through his mind when his heart gave out.

"I love you, pa, rest in peace." I bow down and pay my respects, holding my hands in prayer over his body, praying for his soul and eternal peace. Then I move away and light a candle for him that I place beside the ones already burning brightly.

As I walk away, a darkness descends upon my soul because he is gone. He was the person the entire family orbited around, and our loss is great.

Mama smiles sadly as I pass and whispers, "Go and rest, Alexei. Your brothers will be arriving throughout the day. Bring your guest to meet me in one hour's time."

"You don't have to…"

She holds up her hand. "I insist."

She turns away and heads to the casket and Ana says softly, "She needs a distraction. Your companion will prove a convenient one."

I sigh and as I make to leave, she reaches out and touches my arm. "This woman."

"Serena." I say her name, loving how it curls around my heart.

"You like her?" Ana stares at me with a hopeful expression and I roll my eyes. "I like her, but that's where it ends. We are not together, we are strangers. She is good company that will disappear when she reaches her destination."

I turn to leave, and she whispers, "Then I will pray for you too, Alexei. There are too many Romanovs who prefer to live alone. The only couple who were happy together now find themselves in that same position. Try harder, brother. Find someone who makes you as happy as pa did mama."

She turns away, but her words stay with me. She is right about one thing. The Romanovs are solitary creatures. We let nobody in and if they try, they are rejected. It's easier that way. No regrets and no emotion, just business.

That's all we need. Power, money, and wealth. Not love. Not emotion and definitely not someone else to worry about because it hurts too much when they leave.

CHAPTER 18

SERENA

*A*s soon as my attendants leave, I take a deep breath and really look around. The house is amazing and far too grand for guests. It's a work of art in its own right and I appreciate every single exquisite touch. It's obviously not just a vision from a mood board. There are so many personal touches that make me wonder about Alexei's mother. I can *feel* her here. Everywhere I turn because the small family photographs dotted around the space reveal a family who are very close and enjoy one another's company.

I find myself lingering on the ones of Alexei. He is so handsome and so commanding, even through the camera lens.

I am curious about this family. His brothers are much the same as him and he wasn't kidding when he told me his mother had her hands full. There is one small girl with them. Beautiful and happy. Her eyes sparkle as she is surrounded by her brothers, and it warms my heart. I understand what that's like. To be the center of a family. Surrounded by love and protection—sometimes too much, but like me, I'm guessing she wouldn't want it any other way.

A sudden movement startles me and as I turn, my heart flutters when I see Alexei leaning against the doorjamb watching me.

He shifts off and prowls toward me and takes the silver frame from my hand and smiles.

"My sister Anastasia. We call her Ana. It's a lot less of a mouthful."

He points to the boys beside him. "That's Mikhail. He's a cruel bastard and has never been any different."

I shiver as the eyes that stare out from the frame at me appear to know all my secrets and it appears that Mikhail was born to the life he lives now. There is no emotion in those eyes and just a grave expression, daring anyone to challenge him, something they would regret, I'm sure.

He points to another image. "This is Valentin. He doesn't say much and is a stranger most of the time. Don't expect polite conversation from any of them. They don't know how."

"Your family is much like mine, Alexei."

I say, experiencing a sudden homesickness for my own. "They don't wear emotion well, but I can tell there is a deep love for you all in these photographs."

I point to the one of two older people and note the pain intensify in his eyes. "My mother and father. They were devoted to one another. I am worried for her now he has gone."

"I understand. It must be a huge shock for you all."

I say sadly. "When my own father died, I had a very different reaction to yours and I wonder what that makes me."

He tilts my face to his and stares into my eyes, causing me to falter slightly and then I say with a shrug, "I was happy he died. You must think I'm a monster."

His thumb rubs against my lips and his eyes are almost hypnotizing me as they draw me in and hold me hostage.

"Your father was not a good man, it's obvious." He says with a deep growl.

"He didn't deserve to live if he ordered a hit on his own children. He was a monster."

"You got that right." My eyes fill with tears, and I hate how weak he makes me. Most of the time, I hide away from emotion for a very good reason. I don't let it in, knowing it will destroy me.

Alexei sighs. "You should call your family and tell them you are safe."

"You're probably right."

He takes my hand and as we walk through the magnificent house, I hate that I picture us living here together. When did I start thinking of him this way? He is meant to be a passing fancy. An experience that will be my own personal secret and a delicious memory to look back on when shit happens. Now I'm planning a fucking future with him in this house. I am delirious so I harden my heart and say with a sigh.

"You're right. I'll call my brother, Killian. He is probably going out of his mind by now."

We reach a comfortable sitting room and as I take a seat by the window, Alexei says, "Would you like me to go?"

"No. You're good." I smile because it is good with him by my side. It doesn't make me feel so lonely, and I smile as he sits on the couch and pulls out his own phone.

I take a deep breath and prepare myself for my brother because, unlike my grandfather, he doesn't choose his words carefully.

"Serena."

His low growl causes my heart to beat a little faster and I say as calmly as I can.

"Killian. There's been a change of plan."

"Where are you?"

He doesn't waste time with pleasantries, and I detect an unusual sense of urgency in his voice.

"Russia."

I exhale sharply. "Don't ask me to explain. We don't have time for that, but I just want to reassure you that I'm safe and will resume my journey as soon as possible."

"Serena." His voice is low and crawls through my blood like a deadly virus. There is a warning hidden behind my name, and my skin prickles with alarm.

"You should know there is a hit on you."

I almost drop the phone but say half laughing, "Isn't there always?" I try to make light of it, but inside I am breaking apart.

"We learned of it before you took your trip. It was decided you were better off not knowing and would conduct your visit in ignorance, giving us time to deal with it."

"But they followed me. Is that what you're saying, Kill?"

I am so angry because once again they are cutting me out of the loop because they don't believe I'm capable of looking after myself.

"We don't know, but the fact there was a paid assassin on your flight, swapped at the last minute, makes that a distinct possibility."

"So, what are you saying, Kill?"

I steady my voice, fearing the worst and he says in a low voice that takes no shit, *"Stay there. I will send Shade and the company jet to bring you home."*

"Like fuck you will!" I yell, knowing this is not the best reaction in the world, and Alexei glances up from his phone with concern.

"Serena!" Kill says calmly and I hiss, "Don't you dare send Shade. I am not a child, Kill. I'm a Vieri just as much as you are and I'm telling you that I can deal with my own shit."

I am so incensed, and say icily. "I will be the judge of what is best for me, so tell me what I need to know, and I'll decide where I go from here."

I am fuming, out of control and have lost all reasonable thought, and it doesn't help that my fucking brother is calmness personified.

"All we discovered is there is a hit on you. Trust no one and protect yourself. Mom is waiting for you, and you'll be safe with her, but you need to get there first. Shade can get you there, Serena, and deal with the woman who was paid to kill you. You may be a Vieri, but you are not on your own. There are three of us and only a fool wouldn't use every weapon they have."

I realize he's right and I don't know why I'm making a scene, but I expect it's because this was my one shot at freedom. It's not turning out well at all and if my brother arrives, Alexei will be off the hook. If I'm honest with myself, he is the reason I want to do this alone because all the time he feels the need to protect me, the adventure continues.

However, circumstances have changed, and he is in no position to offer me the same level of help he intended and so, with a sigh, I say in defeat. "Okay. I'll wait for your instruction."

I cut the call because I'm liable to say something I will regret. I know I'm being a brat, but I hate being passed over all the time. I'm a woman and don't have the same position in our family business that my brothers enjoy. I thought I had come to terms with that. It appears I was wrong.

CHAPTER 19

ALEXEI

*F*uck my life. Everything was going so well until it unraveled around me. Now I'm facing something I hoped to avoid. Serena informed me she would be leaving with her brother as soon as he landed, and she was instructed to be at the airport and ready when they arrived. He will text her the estimated time of arrival and she asked if I could call her a cab.

I feel so helpless because I'm in no position to help. My family needs me, and she will soon be with her own. But I don't want to see her leave.

I said nothing and just played it cool, but inside I am tearing myself apart with frustration. Why do I even care? She is a stranger to me, but for some reason I don't want to let her go. I told myself it was to protect her. I was fooling myself. It's purely for selfish reasons. I want to keep her for my pleasure and now I must let her go.

Since the call, it appears a wall is building between us, and I can already tell she is preparing herself to leave, and I must do the same.

She won't even look at me and so, with a heavy heart, I make an excuse to leave and head back to the main house.

"Alexei." I stop as my brother Mikhail heads through the door, his entourage scrambling around him. He crosses the hall, and we embrace as brothers do and he says gruffly, "How is she?"

"Trying to hold it together."

I think of mama and my heart beats faster because she is the only one who matters now. Her future is an undecided one. She is a widow, who has lost a lot more than her husband now. Our older brother Artem will inherit the house and the bulk of the business while the rest of us continue in our roles, making sure that our business prospers.

"Is anyone else here?"

He asks and I nod, "Ana, of course. Valentin has landed and Arman will be here within the hour."

We start to walk toward the chapel and Mikhail says with a hint of anger, "Was it intentional?"

The thought had crossed my mind and I say roughly, "Too early to say. I believe Artem will have planned for an autopsy, but we must make certain it happens when mama is distracted."

"She will agree. If somebody did this, they will pay."

His rough tone sits well with me because, like me, he has already considered the facts. Our father was in good health, had regular check-ups and the hour before he died, he complained about the food.

Mikhail growls, "I have set the wheels in motion to investigate his death. If it was intentional, we are at war."

I nod, my heart sinking as I realize what that means. We come together to make the fuckers pay, and as wars sometimes go, it could be a long one.

We reach the chapel and Mikhail heads straight to mama and Ana whispers, "She's exhausted. She won't leave him."

"I'll see what I can do." I say thoughtfully and as mama leaves Mikhail to pay his respects, I pull her to one side.

"I need your help."

Her eyes widen.

"What can I do?"

"Serena." I am blunt and note how her eyes widen.

"What about her?"

"She's leaving?" For a moment, she stares at me in confusion and then the light shines in her eyes as she whispers, "And you're unhappy about that."

"I am." I play it cool and hate that I'm using Serena to distract my mother from her grief, but I would be lying if I said it wasn't in my own interests too.

She nods and takes my arm.

"Then we should pay her a visit."

Ana smiles and mouths, 'thank you' as we leave her with Mikhail and head back along the path toward the guest house.

"Tell me about her." Mama says softly and I wonder where to even begin.

"She was a stranger a few hours ago who I offered a ride to Australia."

I shrug as she chuckles softly.

"Still playing your games, I see." She rolls her eyes as I shake my head.

"I don't know what you mean." I wink, which causes her face to relax a little, and she grins.

"But this one backfired, perhaps." She says hopefully and I shrug.

"I'm still working that out."

"And she must leave. Why?"

"Her family is mafia, and they want her back."

"Mafia." Mama sighs. "Now I understand. What is her family name?"

"Vieri."

She shakes her head.

"One of the best. I will prepare to be impressed."

She falls silent, and it's as if she is somewhere else entirely, and then she sighs heavily.

"Why is she going to Australia?"

"Her mom lives there."

"And her father?"

"Is dead. Apparently, he ordered a hit on his family, and they got there first."

"And her mom, why is she in Australia?"

Mama doesn't bat an eyelash, reminding me this is normal life for a Romanov.

"She divorced her father and married a man called Joseph Stoner. They live in Australia and, ironically, he is my business there."

Mama stops and stares at me with a confused expression.

"So, Sarah Vieri is married to Joseph Stoner."

"You heard of them?" I'm surprised, although I shouldn't be. Mom only came to live in Russia when she married my father. She is an American by birth and lived there her entire life before she fell in love with him.

"I know them." Her voice has a sad edge to it, and she sighs heavily. "It was so long ago and I'm just a little surprised to hear those names again."

"What do you know of them?"

I'm curious, and mama says with a slight grin. "Enough, Alexei. You see, there is a lot I know, but nobody ever asks. I haven't lived with your father all these years not to have learned how to play the game. This is just what I need right now, but I must ask you to leave us alone."

"Why?" I'm curious but know not to refuse and she just smiles sweetly. "Because women like to gossip, my love, and we don't need an audience. Secrets have a habit of being spilled when the conversation is free, and I apologize in advance for spilling a few secrets of my own."

She laughs softly at my expression, that must be one of confusion. However, she is right. Mama has been a Romanov for more years than she was a Harvey, and I must give her the credit she deserves.

CHAPTER 20

SERENA

*W*hen Alexei left, it gave me a strange feeling inside. I didn't like it. I haven't known him long, but I like him. He's the first man who treated me like a person, not a protected figurehead. Now I must walk away for both our sakes, but I'm hating every minute.

When the door opens, my heart leaps but crashes back to earth when an elegant woman stands there instead of him and says warmly, "You must be Serena."

I smile, realizing immediately this must be Alexei's mother. She has a similarity to Alexei; the same eyes and smile and I note her black dress and sad eyes and my heart reaches out to her.

"Mrs. Romanov. I am sorry for your loss."

I bow my head with respect, and she sighs. "Thank you. I wish we were meeting under happier circumstances, but I heard you are leaving us."

"I shouldn't be here." I say with a sad smile. "You are grieving, and the last thing you need is a visitor intruding on your family's grief."

"I disagree." She points toward the couch.

"Please. Talk to me. I need the distraction."

I'm surprised that she's here at all and, of course, I can refuse her nothing right now, so I do as she asks and perch on the edge of the couch.

She wastes no time and says with a sad smile. "I know your family, Serena."

I stare at her in amazement. "You do?"

"Yes, and one of them personally because I went to college with your Aunt Giselle."

"It's a small world, Mrs. Romanov." I say with a smile, and she nods, her blue eyes piercing as she stares at me with a steadfast look.

"I could never forget her. It was a scandal that was spoken about for years after it happened."

"I don't understand."

There is something telling me I'm about to learn why the Romanovs are so successful because if this is a casual conversation, I'm not a Vieri by birth.

She smiles sympathetically. "She was two years older than me, but we all knew of her. Giselle Vieri was a beautiful woman. She held herself well, almost like a queen, and to us she was."

I remain silent because my aunt has always conducted herself with grace and poise, so I'm not surprised.

"Then a terrible thing happened, and she left college."

I lean forward. "What happened?"

"I'm sorry, my dear, I'm speaking out of turn."

She smiles apologetically, and I fix her with a firm expression of my own.

"Mrs. Romanov, it's obvious you came here to tell me this, so we may as well get on with it."

I hate how abrupt I sound, but I'm not one to mess around and to my surprise, she laughs out loud.

"Now I can see why my son likes you so much."

"He hardly knows me." I say with a wry smile, and she leans forward and says in a lower voice, "I know my son, Serena, and women haven't featured much in his life. He fools around and never brings anyone home and I'm aware of what he's like, what he's capable of and when I heard he was bringing you with him, it gave me hope."

"He didn't have a choice. I'm sorry, he was just being kind."

I try to tell her how it is, but she shakes her head.

"No. Alexei isn't a kind man, Serena. Everything he does is for his own gain. If he didn't want you here, you wouldn't be."

I say nothing, but inside my heart is fluttering. To be needed is the greatest gift anyone could give me because I have been alone my entire life. The fact he brought me here means a lot, but it changes nothing.

I decide to change the subject and say sharply, "I'm sorry, Mrs. Romanov, but I would really like to listen to the memory you have of my aunt."

"Of course." She straightens up and fixes me with a look I can't place, and then she says softly, "You are a lot like my husband, Serena. You don't mess around and like the facts. Andrei would have admired that about you. He was the same, and I learned a lot through him. It appears that comes naturally to you, and I admire you for it."

She smiles and then says with a sigh.

"It's not a happy story, I'm afraid, but I have a feeling it's one you very much need to hear."

"Me?"

I'm confused, and she nods, her eyes gleaming as she takes a trip down memory lane.

"There was a party on campus. There always was, but this one is memorable for one reason. The next day Giselle Vieri returned home and never came back."

"Why?"

I'm intrigued and she sighs. "There was a lot of alcohol and drugs and things started to get out of hand. Giselle was a beautiful woman and attracted attention. That night, it was the wrong kind. She became the target for a group of guys who belonged to the worst kind of fraternity. They were out of control and believed they were invincible. Sadly, for Giselle, her reputation as an ice queen did her no favors, and they trapped her in one of the rooms, and well …"

"Well, what?" My blood has turned to ice as Mrs. Romanov shakes her head. "They raped her, Serena. Every damn one of them."

I have no words and stare at her in shock. Just thinking of what my aunt went through breaks me and she leans forward and stares at me hard. "The guys who did it came from powerful families who always bought their way out of trouble. In this case, they didn't get the chance."

"What happened?"

I almost can't breathe, and she laughs softly. "Your grandfather happened, Serena. Word around campus was Giselle told him everything, and he took them out one by one. They never made it to graduation and the official reason was they were excluded. Nothing was ever said, but we all knew they disappeared off the face of the earth. Five lives cut short because they messed with the wrong family."

"I'm guessing you understand what that's like, Mrs. Romanov." I say with a knowing smile, and she nods. "Of course. It's what families like ours do. They pull together and protect."

"But why are you telling me this?"

"Because the story doesn't end there."

"Go on." I lean forward, my heart racing.

"I met your aunt several years later. She was married to Carlos Matasso at the time, and her friend Catherine was married to Joseph Stoner."

"My mom's Joseph Stoner?"

I don't believe it, and she nods.

"They were a tight group. They did everything together, and we all knew the kind of business the men were involved in.

"But Joseph lives in Australia; he always did. It must have been someone else."

I'm not sure Mrs. Romanov has got this right, but she says with conviction. "It was the same man. His wife Catherine was the love of his life and then she died in an accident. Her car ran off the road and tumbled down a cliff. She never survived. Joseph was heartbroken and returned to Australia, but they kept in touch. At least that's what Andrei told me when I questioned him about them one day."

"Them?" I can't take this all in and she says lightly, "I overheard him mention Joseph Stoner and asked if it was the same man. I told him what I knew, and he divulged something that I never forgot."

"What?"

"That Giselle Vieri had a child. It's why she left college and never returned."

"But she has never had children. Even with Uncle Carlos."

Mrs. Romanov shakes her head. "I don't know about that, but apparently, the child died in childbirth. Giselle made a deal with her father. In return for his help in disposing of her attackers, she would marry Carlos Matasso as arranged to strengthen the Vieri mafia with an alliance."

My head hurts with information overload and I say quickly, "This is a lot to absorb but I still don't know why it concerns me now?"

"Because Andrei told me that Giselle Matasso has been running rings around your family for years. Stoner is a man with a loose tongue when he drinks, and he bragged about his relationship with Giselle Matasso and how evil she was. That she hated her family and her sole aim in life was to bring them down because they ruined her life. She was unhappy in her marriage and blamed her father for arranging it. She saw your father have everything she believed should have been hers. A family, a loving marriage, and the family business. So, she set your father up to cheat and made certain your mother found out. She introduced her to Stoner, and he seduced her to break up her brother's happy family."

"I don't believe you." I stare at her in horror because my aunt is a Vieri first and foremost. She's family and we work together, not against one another.

Mrs. Romanov moves beside me and takes my hands and whispers, "I'm telling you this for your own good. Sometimes the people closest to us wield the sharpest knife. Find your aunt and fear Joseph Stoner. They do *not* have your best interests at heart and if you are searching for the enemy, it could be the enemy within."

She stands and says sadly, "I like you, Serena, and I'm hopeful things work out for you."

She turns to leave, and I stand quickly and say, "Thank you."

She turns and I smile. "I appreciate your honesty, even though it was hard to hear. Thanks for the heads up though. I'll take it from here."

"I know you will, Serena." She flashes me a sad smile. "You're a strong woman. Just be stronger than your aunt."

She leaves me standing helplessly as I watch her go. Everything I thought I knew has been scrubbed through with a big red pen.

As the conversation starts to register, my heritage takes over, leaving a cold fury inside. Knowledge is a powerful weapon when you're fighting a war and this time it's personal.

CHAPTER 21

ALEXEI

*T*ension surrounds us as we wait at the private airfield for the Vieri jet to land. Whatever mama said to Serena didn't help my situation because I returned to find her even more distracted than before.

There is a sadness to her that I share, and I'm guessing we are both dealing with our own shit in much the same way.

I'm surprised when her small hand finds mine when the bright lights of an aircraft materialize from the clouds and she whispers, "Thank you for the best experience of my life."

"Same."

I squeeze her hand hard, hating the distance between us already, and she says with a deep sigh. "For once in my life I felt free. I walked away from the baggage I usually carry and experienced something I probably never will again. I took a chance on you, Alexei, and you didn't let me down. And just for the record, I would definitely travel with your airline again."

She turns and the light in her eyes makes me smile. She is so beautiful, and I can't help reaching out and grasping her face, staring into those beautiful eyes and whispering, "You can travel with me anytime, Serena. There will always be a seat for you on my aircraft."

"A seat?" She shakes her head, the tears brimming in her eyes. "I kind of hoped for one of those flat beds. I like to travel in comfort."

"That goes without saying."

I bend down and kiss her sweet lips, and it's like coming home. My heart leaps inside me and I have an incredible urge to lock the door and drive away with her by my side. The fact she's leaving isn't sitting well with me and imagining her out there with an assassin hot on her trail isn't the best feeling in the world.

She pulls back and rests her head against mine and whispers, "I never understood the term hating goodbyes. Why does this one feel so final?"

"Because there are many unspoken words between us, tiger. We never got to play our game to the end."

The jet screeches overhead and she sighs. "This is it, Alexei. Reality has landed."

"Serena..." I say huskily, and she shakes her head. "Don't make any promises, any plans, or any declarations, Alexei. We both know circumstances may dictate otherwise. Let's leave it here. You have obligations and so do I. Maybe one day our paths will cross again, but I won't hold you to that. At least I have a reminder though, thank you for that."

She grins as she refers to the rose on her ass and I laugh softly. "Just think of me as the thorn in your ass, tiger."

"That's one way of putting it."

We both watch the jet taxi off the runway, and I note the black and silver of their family jet. It is nowhere near as large as the Romanov one, but impressive all the same. We come from two similar worlds, and I hope this is not the end for us, merely a bump in the road.

As the door opens and my guard stands patiently waiting, I

switch emotion off and say firmly, "Come, little one. Your next adventure is waiting for you."

As we retrieve her bag from the trunk, I hate every second of this long goodbye. It shouldn't matter to me, but it does. What turned out as a wild adventure and nothing more, has turned into an experience I am struggling to forget.

*　*　*

WE STAND at the foot of the steps and the door opens and several guards head down them, causing Serena to groan.

"Fuck my life."

I chuckle softly as one of them stares at me with suspicion and nods with respect. "Miss Vieri, Mr. Romanov."

He reaches for her bag, and we glance past him as a man appears and Serena groans. "It appears that my brother wants to meet you."

I stare with interest at the man heading toward us and it's immediately noticeable he is the one in charge around here. Dressed all in black with a scowl on his face, he heads toward us with an air of danger surrounding him.

His first thought is for his sister, and I watch as he scans her face with concern, checking that she's okay, and she smiles coolly. "Shade. It's good to see you."

I'm surprised when he reaches out and pulls her against him hard, his arms wrapping around her as he holds her against his chest, burying his face in her hair and whispering something I can't quite make out.

For a second she sags against him, and I hate that I have lost her already and still holding her in his arms, he stares at me with an expression that tells me if I've fucked with her, I'm dead.

I regard him coolly and he says in a husky growl, "Thank you for looking after my sister, Mr. Romanov. I won't forget it."

I nod, masking my emotion as I have been trained to do. It

appears we all went to the same school for that because there is nothing but cool detachment from all three of us now.

He pulls back from Serena and stares at her hard and says with a satisfied nod, "Come. We must be airborne within ten minutes to keep our arrival slot."

He stands to one side to allow her to pass him and as she turns, I watch the mask slip and desperation replace cool indifference. Her eyes fill with tears, and, to my surprise, she pulls away from him and moves toward me, reaching out and hugging me hard. Much like her brother's, my arms fold around her and I whisper, "This isn't the end of our show, little one, it's merely the interval."

She stares up at me and smiles. "I hope so, Alexei. You still owe me thirteen hours of adventure."

She grins as she backs away and then turns and runs up the stairs of the aircraft without looking back, leaving me with her brother, who stares at me with a hooded expression and says darkly, "She is my sister, Mr. Romanov. I'm sure you understand what happens if I discover something I don't like."

I return his dark expression and growl, "Mr. Vieri, I don't miss the threat in your statement. I can assure you I only have Serena's best interests at heart and as a brother myself, I understand your concerns. I am not the threat to Serena's life. You should look closer to home for that, and I want to offer you my assistance should you need my help in dealing with that."

I nod toward the aircraft, hating that she has disappeared into it already, and I sigh.

"Serena will fill you in. I wish you luck and safe travels."

He stares at me hard and I note the slightly crazed expression of a man who lives in chaos most of his life. We all share that look. Our lives are hard, and money is the honey coating the sour interior. Shade Vieri deals with the madness daily and I understand what that must be like. My brother Mikhail has the same chaos in his eyes, and it makes me feel better knowing Serena has him beside her as she heads off to deal with something only a family can.

He nods and sprints back up the steps and, as the guards follow, I sigh inside. I hate this shit on a good day, but right now, watching it take Serena away from me, I would sacrifice it all for a few more hours with her.

CHAPTER 22

$\mathcal{S}$hade is staring at me, and I say irritably, "Just say it."

"What, princess?"

"What you are dying to ask."

"That man."

"Alexei." I stare at him with a hard expression.

"What are your feelings for him?"

He doesn't waste words and I shrug. "He helped me. I'm grateful, that is all."

He leans forward. "Are you telling me or yourself because I'm not buying it?"

For some reason, it makes me laugh, and I lean back and stare at him fondly. "Thanks for coming." I say with a grateful smile, and he nods. "I will always come for you, princess. You can be assured of that."

The flight attendant brings us some refreshment. A coffee for me and Shade's customary bourbon.

It momentarily distracts us and as we lean back with our drinks in hand, I stare at the disappearing country and sigh inside. It feels wrong leaving Alexei, although it shouldn't. I should be more concerned about what's waiting for me and so I say with a heavy sigh, "Mrs. Romanov told me a story you may be interested in."

He says nothing, but his eyes flash as I fill him in, and I wait for his reaction.

If anything, I don't get one except his eyes darken and he says roughly, "Do you believe her?"

"She had no reason to lie, Shade. She was warning me."

He leans back and says with a ragged breath, "Fuck."

"Do you think nonno knows?"

I am fearful of that, and he shakes his head. "I guess not. We both witnessed his reaction to our own father when he betrayed us all. I'm guessing Aunt Giselle would suffer the same fate."

"This is terrible. Why would she try to bring down her own family? It doesn't make sense."

I am so angry and my eyes flash as I stare at my brother, who has settled into his usual cold rage and says in an emotionless voice.

"Before we say anything to him, I'm guessing we should pay our dear aunt a visit."

"What about my visit to mom?"

Shade shrugs. "The choice is yours. Visit mom and discover the facts from her first and risk Stoner alerting Aunt Giselle and taking away our element of surprise, or charter a different course and head to the Hamptons and pay our dear aunt an unexpected visit."

I weigh up the options, knowing I have a difficult choice to make. I want to do both, but realize if this is to play out properly, we should turn this bird around and head back home. However, mom is my priority now and I say firmly, "My trip continues. They have no idea we know anything about this and won't be on their guard. I will gather information and report back and when my trip is over, I will return home and we can deal with Aunt Giselle as a family."

"If that is your wish, princess, I agree."

He appears thoughtful. "I'll return home after a few days. Mom has been told you missed your flight because I decided to visit. She won't think anything of that, it makes sense, and I will occupy Stoner with a business deal he would be a fool to refuse."

Shade taps his fingers on the armrest and is thinking hard. Then he says with a grin, "I'll fill Killian in on the situation. He will gather the information we need on Aunt Giselle and investigate the facts. It's up to him to decide if nonno needs to be informed."

He stretches out and yawns. "Fuck, I need to sleep. I suggest you take advantage of this journey and do the same. You look as if you could use it."

He winks and I growl, "Fuck you, Shade."

I move away and head to one of the bedrooms with a stupid grin on my face. Is it that obvious? Apparently so, because sleep hasn't really featured much in my journey so far and he is right, I could sure use some now.

* * *

I MUST PASS out because the first thing I'm aware of is when the bed dips and my first thought is Alexei.

Sadly, it's just my maniacal brother, and he tickles me awake.

"Fuck off, Shade."

"Just so you know, Serena. You're shit company. Remind me never to travel with you again."

I toss the pillow at him and stretch. "What time is it?"

"Landing time."

I stare at him in shock because it's as if I've only just got into bed and he grins. "You slept for eight hours. You must have needed it."

I shrug. "I did."

I swing back the covers and head to the bathroom, saying over my shoulder, "You can show yourself out."

"Is there something you want to tell me, princess?"

The tone of his voice stops me in my tracks, and I turn, noting the thunderous expression on his face. "What?"

"You left this behind."

I swallow hard when I see him holding the bandage that must have fallen off my ass, and he cocks his head. "What's this?"

"None of your business."

I turn to go, knowing he won't be happy with that response and his voice is cold and laced with threats as he hisses, "Then I will have to ask the man you traveled with why there is blood in this bandage. Did he hurt you?"

I don't miss the threat in his voice, or the tension between us, and I turn to face him and scowl. "If you must know, I got a tattoo. No big deal, you have several."

I turn and flash him a view, and the surprise on his face makes me giggle.

"When?" He is shocked and I shrug.

"You can get anything on the Romanov jet. A massage, a gourmet meal, a movie, oh and a tattoo. Apparently, they all do it to pass the time."

"I won't ask what else you did to pass the time." Shade sighs and then says with interest, "Can I see it?"

"If you like." I don't have a problem flashing my ass at my brother and I move closer so he can appreciate Alexei's art.

"It's good." He sounds impressed. "Small but delicate and warns of danger if touched. I like it."

"I may get another."

He shrugs. "Tattoo your whole body if it makes you happy. I'm not one to talk."

I sit beside him on the bed and lift his hand, tracing the intricate design that covers his hand.

"Did this hurt?"

"Not really. A little pain brings a lot of pleasure if it's done right."

I change the subject before my expression gives a lot more away than I'm happy with.

"Tell me about Allegra."

I'm curious about Shade's new girlfriend.

"Is she mentally disturbed?" I say with a slight grin, and he nods. "Of course. I wouldn't be interested if she wasn't."

It makes me laugh because my brother is the craziest person I have ever met, which is a good thing considering he runs the mafia side of our organization. I smile and drop his hand and am surprised when he catches my hand and says in a whisper, "If you like the Russian, tell him."

"Alexei." My heart beats faster as I think about him and Shade smiles. "Don't play games with your emotions, Serena. Who knows how long we have left in the game? You may as well enjoy it while it lasts."

"When did you grow up, Shade?" I tease, but his words hit home. The fact there's a hit on me makes them meaningful and I bend down and kiss his cheek, and whisper, "Thanks. I'll bear that in mind."

This time he lets me go and as I shower and change ready for landing, I really hope I get the chance to see Alexei again and see if what I'm feeling now is real, or just wishful thinking.

CHAPTER 23

SERENA

*I*t's as if the last two days never happened. We arrive in Sydney and yet this time I don't need anyone to meet me. Typical of Shade, there are enough cars waiting to stage a coup and as I sit beside him in the third one, I'm a little sad I never got to arrive like everyone else.

As we head off to Vaucluse, I am in two minds about going at all because I may not like what I discover.

Shade is scrolling through his phone, and I interrupt him. "Do you think mom knows about Stoner and Aunt Giselle?"

"I'm not sure." He stops scrolling. "It will be interesting to find out."

"How will we broach the subject? It's not something you can drop into everyday conversation."

'You'll find a way. You're good at that shit."

He shakes his head and I note the murderous gleam in his eye as he growls, "Leave Stoner to me. That greedy, money grabbing bastard is certain to fall into my trap. I almost hope he's to blame for it all because I would welcome taking him apart limb from limb."

"You should seek help for your anger issues, Shade." I grin as he shrugs. "Where's the fun in that? What can I say? I love my job."

It takes us about an hour to reach Stoner's ranch and I plague Shade with questions about his new girlfriend, Allegra. If anything, I pity her having to deal with his shit daily, but I don't believe I have ever seen him as happy as he is now.

As we sweep through the gates of their fifty-acre ranch, I hope with all my heart that Mrs. Romanov was wrong. This is the only bit of normal in my life that I really don't want to lose.

* * *

WE PULL up in the courtyard and my heart leaps when I see my mom standing by the door with a broad smile on her face.

As soon as the door opens, I can't get out of it quickly enough and as I fall into her arms, everything is right with the world.

"Serena. It's so good to see you, honey." She pulls me in for a hug and she smells so nice. Flowers, baking and mom. My favorite scent in the world.

Shade isn't far behind me, and she hugs him hard and says happily, "This is such a nice surprise. I've missed you so much."

She stares at us both with a tearful smile and laughs joyfully. "Come inside. I want to hear everything and don't miss anything out."

She links her arms in mine and Shade follows us behind and it crosses my mind that Mrs. Romanov must have been wrong about Stoner. Mom is obviously happy, which gives me no reason at all to doubt that he loves her.

* * *

WE HEAD inside the huge ranch that always appears warm and cozy despite its size, and I plant myself on the oversized couch and groan with pleasure.

"This feels so good."

Mom grins happily and then smiles as her housekeeper brings in a tray of refreshment, which I am grateful for.

When we are settled, she stares at us with a sad shake of her head. "I was sorry to hear about your father. How are you both?"

We maintain blank expressions and I say guardedly, "It was a shock, but not unexpected."

She nods. "It was always a possibility. He was so reckless."

"Are you okay, mom?" I stare at her with concern, noticing a few lines that weren't there before and a sadness in her eyes that definitely isn't through grieving our father's untimely death.

"I just worry about you all. It's hard being here, not knowing if the next phone call will break my heart. I thought when I left, I would walk away from the pain. If only it has intensified."

"How?" I lean forward as she smiles bravely. "I am so far away and if anything happened, I wouldn't be there which breaks my heart."

"It was a choice you made." Shade interrupts coldly and my mother winces at his words.

"You're right, Shade. I did choose to walk away, and circumstances made this the place I ran to."

"Stoner, you mean." Shade doesn't mince his words and mom sighs.

"You can't help who you fall in love with. I was in a vulnerable state of mind and Joe helped me through. It was inevitable we would fall in love."

"Why?" He shakes his head. "Kyle helps me out of many impossible situations, but it doesn't mean I love him."

I can't help laughing because Kyle is Shade's consigliere, and they are more like brothers than associates.

Mom smiles. "You know what I mean. Joe helped pick up the pieces when your father, well, cheated on me and it meant a lot."

"From what I remember, dad cheated on you your entire married life. Why was one more so different?"

I understand why my brother is being deliberately cruel because anger can bring revelation and mom is no different as she snaps, "We all know Benito cheated on me, Shade. Perhaps the last one was the final nail in our marriage. There is only so much a woman can stand and it became an impossible situation."

"What happened?" I say softly, my good cop to Shade's bad one, and she says with a pained expression, "I found them in our bed. They were asleep at the time, but it was obvious what went on. She was one of the maids. It wasn't the first time he slept with the staff, but it was the first time in our bed. It was disrespectful and belittled me and I had enough."

"So how did Stoner come into it?" Shade says in a softer voice that obviously works because mom relaxes a little.

"I had nowhere to go, and your Aunt Giselle was a good friend to me and offered me her penthouse in the city. Joseph had an apartment in the same building, and we met in the elevator a few times. I knew of him through parties at the house. He was a business associate of your father's and a good friend with Giselle and Carlos."

She smiles. "We got talking, and he invited me out for dinner. He was a good listener and made me laugh. It was…" She smiles wistfully. "The first time I felt like a normal woman."

I can so relate to that, and my heart reaches out to her. I understand what that's like. The yearning for normality in a crazy fucked-up world and I'm not surprised she fell for Stoner if he gave her the opportunity.

"Talking of Joe." She smiles as the door slams and the man himself heads into the room and shouts, "What the fuck is going on? I couldn't even get through my own gate; some guy stopped me and …"When he notices Shade watching him, he falters momentarily but quickly recovers and smiles.

"Shade, Serena. I might have known. I only expected Serena. Now we have double the pleasure."

He moves across to mom and kisses her cheek and then offers

his hand to Shade, who shakes it politely, keeping it short and sweet.

He moves across to me and kisses me on both cheeks, and I detect the scent of alcohol on his breath.

He shakes his head with concern. "I don't know where we'll put all those men?"

Shade adds, "We only need three extra rooms. The rest will wait on the aircraft."

"So, you're not saying long, then?" I sense the relief in his voice and Shade shrugs. "Long enough to put some business your way, then I'm leaving. Duty calls."

"And you, Serena?" Stoner fixes me with an enquiring stare, and I smile. "Three weeks was the plan. I hope that still stands."

"Of course it does." Mom interrupts and smiles warmly.

"Anyway, you must be exhausted. I'll show you to your rooms. We can catch up over dinner."

We leave Stoner and follow her out and as we close the door, she whispers, "He is preoccupied at the moment. There's an important meeting he's been preparing for with a Russian family. Once it's over, he'll be more relaxed."

My heart flutters at the mention of Alexei and I maintain my cool and say evenly, "When is the meeting?"

"In three days' time, I believe." She shakes her head. "It was meant to be tomorrow, but there was an unfortunate emergency that put it back. Apparently, a lot is riding on the success of this meeting. We stand to make a great deal of money if they sign the contract."

I say nothing but my heart is racing because in a few days' time Alexei will be here, and for some reason everything looks a lot better than it did five minutes ago.

CHAPTER 24

ALEXEI

I hate leaving my family, but mom insisted. My father's funeral was yesterday, and I'm still reeling from the effects of it. As expected, it was a large gathering and was executed in the usual Romanov way. Organized with a meticulous attention to detail that was the result of a well-oiled machine.

We had some tests run on the body through a private channel and are waiting for the results of that. Mom never found out because we kept her from visiting my father's coffin while they were carried out. The results will take a week and will go straight to Artem as the head of the family.

If my father was murdered, we will soon know and take the necessary steps taken to bring about justice for our family.

Mikhail will be accompanying me to Australia. Mom insisted we carry on with business because it was what our father would have wanted. Artem and Ana are remaining with her, and Valentin is returning to Europe and Arman is heading to America. We will come together forty days after his death to remember him with a lavish dinner. Until then, it is business as usual.

My journey is very different this time, as Mikhail occupies

most of my time by talking business while I tattoo our father's name above his heart. I'm surprised there is any room for more because he is completely covered across his torso and arms, his back and shoulders not quite so decorated.

"I've checked the schedule." He says with a growl as the needle digs a little deeper.

"The crew leave in two days for home. We don't have long."

I agreed to accompany Mikhail when he questions Regina. We need to discover who her target is and will deal with the result of that accordingly.

"This woman." Mikhail says gruffly.

"Serena?"

"You like her?"

"Not you as well." I roll my eyes. "Mom can't stop talking about her and it's obviously rubbed off on you. I gave her a ride, and I didn't know who she was until we took off. It made it interesting."

I grin, remembering the last tattoo I inked.

"The Vieris are a powerful family." Mikhail reminds me and I shrug.

"Then we have something in common."

I stare at him with interest. "What about you? Are you any closer to making mama's dreams come true?"

"Of course not. I'm not interested in one woman. Too much trouble."

"I agree."

I dismiss my growing feelings for Serena because I'm not ready to admit them even to myself, and I change the subject rapidly.

"What are your plans after Australia?"

I'm curious because Mikhail is a closed book even to family, and he shrugs. "I have some business in America. There is a group threatening the oil refinery. Some green activists who are about to learn they don't always get their own way."

I laugh softly because I can just imagine the shock on their faces when my brother and his men head their way. I'm guessing they won't be protesting much longer, and our business can carry on operating without any unwelcome distractions.

As soon as the tattoo is done, Mikhail heads off to eat and I decide to freshen up and then prep for my meeting with Stoner and if I discover he is responsible for the hit on Serena, he will learn how ruthless I can be.

* * *

We land in the evening and Mikhail jumps into the car with me and the rest head off to the family property in Sydney. We own houses around the world with the latest security measures in place and rooms to accommodate our staff and guests. We live a life of great riches and our sole aim in it is to make more. However, I am fast realizing there are some riches you can't buy with money and for a man who usually gets what he wants, it's a hard pill to swallow.

We head to the Regency hotel where the airline staff stays on their stopover and rather than head through the main entrance, the driver takes us via the underground car park.

We already obtained the security code to enter, and as we step into the elevator, I set my mood accordingly.

Mikhail, as always, appears ready to take on a small army and yet our victim is one fragile woman who uses that as her strength.

Regina Silver is good at what she does because of it. Nobody suspects her, and she uses cunning rather than strength to get the job done.

Mikhail discovered she occupies room 605. There is always someone happy to take a bribe for a decent amount of money and the receptionist in this hotel was no exception. The security cameras were dealt with, courtesy of a call from the company who provided them. A routine check was the excuse, but they have been tampered with to show the same image on a loop until our mission is complete. Mikhail has a duplicate key card, and we are going there now while Regina is at dinner with the crew. Our surveillance is tight, and we leave nothing to chance and, as we slip into her room under the protection of darkness, we take our positions and wait.

* * *

HALF AN HOUR later it's showtime and a text on Mikhail's phone alerts us she is coming, and we take up our positions with Mikhail behind the door and me in the bathroom.

I hear voices outside and Regina says softly, "Thanks guys, see you in the morning."

The door opens and as it slams, I hear a squeal, which is my cue to enter the room.

Mikhail has his large hand flat against her mouth and has secured her wrists behind her back as she struggles to defend herself using her legs. With a smack, he brings her down and I register the pain in her eyes as he damages something in her knee.

He works fast, and she is soon tied up on the chair, her hands tied behind her back and her ankles to the chair legs. He has stuffed a rag into her mouth so she can't speak, and her anger is pouring off her in furious waves.

"I thought it was you, Regina."

I say smoothly, sitting on the edge of the bed as I admire Mikhail's handiwork.

"I'm a little disappointed, though."

I shake my head as she glares at me with intent. "I thought you were better than this. I would want my money back if I had paid you as a hitman. It was too easy to restrain you."

Mikhail laughs and pulls her head back by her hair, causing

the tears to spill from her eyes as I lean forward and say evenly, "Why were you on my flight from Chicago?"

Her eyes widen because it's obvious she didn't know I was meant to be there, which tells me I wasn't her intended victim.

I say in a whisper, "My brother will let you speak, but if you scream, he will snap your neck before you take your next breath."

Her eyes are wide and full of fear, and I nod to Mikhail, who tears the gag from her mouth, causing her to gulp for air.

"I would start talking, Regina." I say coolly and she hisses, "I was called out. It's my job. I don't know what you're talking about."

There is a possibility she is telling the truth, but as we had eyes on her since she landed, we know her movements and she hasn't been visiting the usual tourist haunts. If anything, she has been familiarizing herself with places Serena's family visit and was followed out to Stoner's ranch where she apparently spent an afternoon walking the perimeter.

I lean back and say with a sigh.

"Don't treat me as a fool, Regina. We've been watching you since you arrived in Sydney. It appears you have developed quite the fascination for Joseph Stoner. I also happen to be meeting him, which makes me wonder if you knew that."

"No!" Her eyes are wide, and she appears fearful. She realizes if I thought for one minute she was after me she wouldn't be leaving this room and so I say evenly, "I will ask you again. Who is your intended victim and who ordered the hit?"

She drops her eyes and Mikhail forces her head up to stare at me and growls, "Answer my brother, because unless you give him the information he is asking for, your career is over, along with your life."

She nods her acceptance and exhales sharply. "Serena Vieri."

My anger is balling like an iron fist inside me as I picture what could have happened if I hadn't intervened, and she groans.

"It was going to be easy. I had some drugs to put in her drink to cause a heart attack."

Mikhail glances at me sharply and I say tightly, "Why?"

She shrugs. "I don't know. They didn't give a reason. I was being paid a shit load of dollars for the easiest hit of my career. The rest doesn't concern me."

I feel my blood actually boiling and snarl, "Who ordered the hit?"

"It was anonymous. It came through the usual email I use, no questions asked, just half up front and the rest on completion. If the hit fails, they get their money back."

"So, you are still planning on making the hit, anyway. That is why you were stalking Stoner's ranch. I'm guessing you planned to get inside and carry it out before your flight back, knowing you don't have long."

I stare at her with a growing hatred as she shrugs. "You understand how it works, Alexei. You've used my services a few times. I'm a professional and I don't want to issue a refund so I do everything I can to deliver. Serena Vieri arrived two days ago, and I only have one more chance tomorrow. It's all arranged, and I'm assured of my success, so everyone's happy."

"Not everyone."

I growl, "I'm guessing Serena Vieri wouldn't be too happy and neither would her family. You are taking a risk even attempting to remove one of them, so I will ask you again, who ordered the hit?"

Her eyes widen as I back her into a corner and as she opens her mouth to speak, Mikhail growls, "The name or die. It's your choice."

He wraps his hands around her neck and whispers darkly, "I will snap your pretty neck in two if you don't give my brother the name."

He increases the pressure on her neck, and she croaks, "Okay. I'll tell you, just keep me out of it."

Mikhail relaxes his hold, and she sighs. "It's not worth dying over. The hit was arranged by Giselle Matasso and Joseph Stoner is my way in."

"How?" I say with deepening anger, and she says angrily, "He ordered some flowers for his wife and I'm the delivery girl. As soon as I get access to the house, I will be shown to the kitchen. There will be four glasses of champagne on the tray waiting and one martini cocktail, which I am to add the poison to and then leave."

"That sounds risky." I glance at my brother. "Anyone could drink it."

She shakes her head. "Apparently, Serena can't stand champagne and the cocktail is her usual drink. They will be celebrating some business deal Joseph is negotiating and nobody will detect the drug because it's untraceable."

"Then why didn't he add the drugs himself?" Mikhail says with confusion. "Why involve you at all?"

She shrugs. "The fuck I know. Like I said, its easy money."

She laughs softly. "That family is one crazy assed pile of shit. I was told to hold off doing it on the flight to avoid the authorities being involved, and it was important that she reached her destination in one piece. It would have been far easier to add it to her drink on the flight over."

Something doesn't add up and I can't put my finger on it. She's right, about the flight over and like my brother, I am wondering why Stoner couldn't add the poison himself.

I have a feeling we're not seeing the full picture here and so I say darkly, "You will carry out your instructions."

Her eyes widen and I snarl, "You will say nothing of our meeting and just report back that you did as instructed and if anyone finds out you told me about this, you will be the next corpse in the mortuary."

She stares at me with a calculating expression, and I can tell she is weighing up the positives of which side to fall on. The fact our reputation is far more ruthless that Giselle's makes her lower her eyes and sigh. "I'll do it. I give you my word."

"Oh, I know you'll do it, Regina."

I laugh softly. "You see, I currently have a contract of my own in place, and it relies on you doing what I say."

"What are you talking about?" Her eyes are wide, and I say with a wicked grin. "That's a very pleasant neighborhood your parents live in. I doubt there is much crime there at all. How shocking it will be when they are found dead in an apparent suicide pact. I wonder what the neighbors will say?"

"Fuck you, Alexei." She yells. "Fuck you! You keep away from my parents or…"

Mikhail grips her neck hard and squeezes, causing her to choke as she gasps for air, and then he releases her and growls, "Now shut the fuck up and do your job. If it goes according to plan, we walk away. What is the saying you Americans use…" he grins. "Oh yes. The ball is now in your court. Decide wisely."

I stand to leave and say pleasantly, "This was nice, wasn't it? Enjoy your flight home, Regina. Stay safe."

As we leave, Mikhail cuts the ties we used to bind her wrists and ankles and we leave without another glance in her direction.

Regina has too much to lose, which is why I am assured of her services. After all, family is everything.

CHAPTER 25

SERENA

*J*don't do excitement. I can't even remember the last time I was excited, but I am now.

Stoner is full of his own self-importance because today he is negotiating a business deal worth millions. At least that's how he puts it. He seems kind of high on life right now after Shade offered him a business deal he couldn't refuse and it was with a heavy heart that I bid farewell to my brother and his guards earlier on today.

I know it was just a smoke screen to bring me here and I hope he didn't give Stoner too much money. Like me, my brothers don't trust him at all and I still to this day don't know what my mom sees in him.

He is arrogant, self-absorbed, and rude. His table manners are disgusting, and he has probably never even set foot in a gym. He is overweight to the point of obese and drinks too much. His hair gave up and left years ago and now he shaves his head, which doesn't suit him.

I also don't appreciate the way he speaks to my mom. He cuts her short in conversations and dismisses anything she says with a roll of his eyes. In his mind, she is only good at hanging off his arm at functions and lying in his bed at night. He gives her limitless credit to amuse herself but doesn't want her opinion on anything. He is most definitely the king of his castle, and she is his reluctant queen.

The more time I spend with them, the more I notice it. If I believed mom was happy before, I know she isn't now. There are the unguarded looks that tell me she despises him. The irritated shake of her head when he holds court at the dinner table. She flinches when he touches her and only appears happy when he's not around. I notice everything and as we take a walk to the stables, I say carefully, "Are things okay with you and Stoner, mom?"

"Why do you ask?" She doesn't look at me and I pull on her arm and say, "Tell me."

She stops and sighs, a disappointed glint in her eye.

"I pray you never find yourself in my position, Serena."

"What position?" I stare at her hard and she sighs.

"One failed marriage was bad enough, but two is careless."

"So, you're unhappy."

"I think I am." She smiles tearfully.

"Joe isn't the man I fell in love with. I'm not naive enough to believe it will always be hearts and flowers, but it's as if he changed when we came here. I put it down to the Australian way. Now he was home, he was the man in charge. He had lots of business to deal with and didn't have as much time for me."

She shrugs and turns to carry on walking.

"I've tried so hard to bring back what I came here with. A partner who enjoyed my company. Who listened when I spoke and only wanted the best for me."

She shakes her head sadly. "He is distant, Serena. He always appears to be somewhere else in his mind and when I ask him about it, well, he gets angry."

"How angry, mom?" My voice is coated in steel, and she turns and says urgently, "I've said too much. You are a Vieri, Serena, and I know what that means. Family is everything to you and your loyalty is admirable. However, there are some things you can't control with violence."

"So he is violent toward you."

"I didn't say that." She seems afraid and backtracks quickly. "Listen. I have spoken out of turn. Forget I even said anything. Just allow me to clear up my own mistakes and learn from them."

She stops and grips my shoulders, staring into my eyes with a hard expression. "Don't be me, Serena. Choose a man who is honorable, kind and would move the sun for you. Don't settle for anything less because it's worth waiting rather than making terrible mistakes along the way."

"You haven't made mistakes, mom." I smile. "You married our father and now you have us. We are your family as much as his and there is nothing we wouldn't do to make you happy. Come back with me to Chicago. Anywhere even. We could buy you a house, somewhere nice and safe, and you could live a normal life away from this shit."

"It's a nice thought, Serena, but I am too far down this road to turn back now. I must deal with it in my own way, and I will— deal with it, I mean."

Mom's eyes flash and it makes me smile. Yes, I may be a Vieri, but I am also part of Sarah Collins, and she has a fire deep inside her I recognize. I should trust her, of course I should, but what daughter wouldn't want vengeance if her mom was unhappy?

As she carries on walking, I caress the ball of burning hatred I have for her husband, and if it was up to me, by the time I leave, she will be free of him.

* * *

WE SPEND the morning riding across their vast acreage, and this is what I love. The freedom, the fresh air and the sunshine beating down on my back. Here I am free of responsibility. I am not accompanied by Connor or one of the other guards. I'm a daughter visiting her mom and this is exactly what I came here for.

We head back to the ranch house for lunch and my heart quickens when I see the car parked outside the entrance. A guard is leaning against the passenger door, smoking a cigarette and talking to the driver of the car behind. Black cars contain black hearts and I hope like hell these belong to the one I can't stop thinking about.

I turn to mom and whisper, "Is this the Russian Stoner has a meeting with?"

Mom nods, a flash of distaste passing across her face.

"Yes. His name is Alexei Romanov and I understand his family is one of the most powerful in Russia. I overheard Joe talking on the phone a few weeks ago. He was excited to have brokered this deal and hopes to be the middleman in a huge diamond operation. Apparently, they will take what we can produce, and that is a very tasty carrot to dangle before a man like Joe."

I can't help feeling elated as I picture Alexei in the same house as me and yet as I glance down at my dusty jodhpurs and bemoan the state of my hair and make-up, I really hope he's still around when I've had the chance to clean up.

"Will they be staying for dinner?" I say casually, disguising my interest in their visitor.

"I think that was the plan." Mom shrugs. "Joe wanted the cook to really go to town to impress them."

She sighs and fixes me with an apologetic look. "I'm sorry, honey. You will be bored to tears and I wouldn't blame you if you swerved dinner and had something in your room."

"On the contrary, mom." I smile happily. "I can't wait."

* * *

IT'S six o'clock and I'm dressed in a red satin dress with matching heels which are the only formal clothes I brought with me. My hair is freshly washed, and my make-up carefully crafted and my nails are as red as the rose Alexei tattooed on my ass. I am so excited to see him again and still can't believe he is here at all.

I wait nervously in the reception room with mom and find myself fidgeting and jumping at any loud noise.

"Are you okay, honey?" Mom appears concerned and I nod, trying to get my breathing under control.

"Of course. I'm just hungry, I guess."

She nods. "Me too. I don't imagine they will be much longer?"

As if on cue, we hear voices and I prepare my mood because I must act as if we are strangers. That was my rule and I wonder if he will remember that.

I hear Stoner's loud voice approaching. "You won't regret this, Alexei. You have chosen the right organization for your business."

As they approach, my heart bangs mercilessly inside me as I detect the low rumble of a Russian accent, but I can't make out the words.

We peer up as they get closer, and my heart actually flutters when I see Alexei walking into the room beside Stoner with Gleb behind him.

Our eyes meet and my heart races when I see the hunger in his match my own. They burn with desire, and it takes all my self-control not to fling myself into his arms and hold on tight.

I've only known him for hours, but it's as if I've known him my entire life and it takes a superhuman effort on my part to smile politely as Stoner makes the introductions.

"Sarah, honey. Come and meet Alexei."

Mom steps forward with a polite smile.

"I'm pleased to meet…"

Stoner cuts her off mid-sentence. "This is her daughter, Serena. She's here visiting her mom."

Alexei stares at me with a polite smile and I take his outstretched hand and say coolly. "Alexei, I'm pleased…"

"Ah, here is Martha with those drinks I promised you, Alexei."

I don't miss the irritated glare Alexei directs at Stoner, which is probably due to his rudeness as he dismisses both me and my mom.

However, Alexei merely steps back and looks with interest as Martha carries a silver tray into the room.

Stoner steps forward and hands a glass of champagne to each of us, and takes the martini cocktail for himself, before raising it in a toast.

"To partnerships. May they be long and powerful ones."

Alexei catches my eyes and raises his glass. "To partnerships."

I echo the words and as I hold the glass to my lips, I'm surprised when Alexei shakes his head slightly and doesn't touch his drink. Gleb does the same and so I lower my glass, unsure what the warning means.

Stoner doesn't notice and just proceeds to talk loudly over everyone, telling Alexei all about his businesses and how powerful he is.

I want to yawn so badly but I don't want to upset my mother, who is doing an extremely good job of holding it together.

After an excruciating thirty minutes of listening to Stoner pontificate, Martha returns to tell us that dinner is served.

CHAPTER 26

ALEXEI

*I*t took every ounce of willpower I possess not to pull Serena into my arms the minute I saw her. My eyes burned with lust when I saw her standing there in that red dress and heels. I am used to the weary traveler, but not the lady. Serena Vieri is every dream I ever had, sugar-coated in evil. There was something so powerful about the way she stared at me as I entered the room. She has a commanding presence, and I couldn't tell what she was thinking. Nobody knows how well we are acquainted and apparently, she wants to keep it that way.

I was interested in meeting her mom. She is like Serena in a lot of ways, beautiful, poised, and elegant, but she lacks the same fire in her eyes.

Perhaps it's years of being dismissed and belittled by Benito Vieri and then by Joseph Stoner. In that short introduction, I could tell she was downtrodden, and I am happy she will soon be free if Regina played her part in this.

As a precaution, I refrained from sipping my drink and made certain Serena heeded my warning. There is nothing I can do about her mother and just hope Regina was telling the truth.

Joseph Stoner is everything I hate in an associate and definitely a man and I hope the poison works its magic soon because I'm likely to end his life myself if he carries on bragging about how powerful he is. A powerful man is that way because of knowledge. When to speak and when to listen. Stoner hasn't read the memo which reveals how little power he actually holds.

As we head into the dining room, he walks by my side spouting off about the exotic places he's traveled to, completely ignoring his wife and Serena, who lag some way behind.

I am aware of every step Serena takes, every word she says and every movement she makes. My entire focus is on her and yet to anybody watching, I have disregarded her completely. Gleb was warned to act as if they are strangers, and he is playing his part perfectly and I'm relying on a different outcome for this evening from the one Stoner intended.

He ignored Gleb for the entire meeting, and it proves to me that I never want to do business with a man like that. I treat everyone with respect and expect the same in return, which is why I'm glad I made the decision to end Joseph Stoner's miserable life.

I'm impatient for the results I was promised and feel a growing sense of anger that I have been double-crossed. Stoner appears perfectly well, and I am already plotting Regina's demise.

We take our seats, and I am placed next to Stoner with Gleb on his other side. Serena is beside Gleb, and I have the pleasure of dining beside her mother. This way I can stare at Serena without drawing attention to it and I am already picturing all the depraved activities I have in mind for her when we are alone.

The starter arrives, shellfish in a Marie rose sauce and as I lift my cutlery, Stoner falls on his like a pig in a trough.

I catch Serena's eyes and smile at the disgust she directs his way as she delicately holds her own fork to her mouth. Gleb is staring at Stoner with revulsion and then catches my eye with a slight shake of his head.

"Mr. Romanov." Sarah distracts my attention and I smile. "Please, call me Alexei."

"Thank you." She smiles. "You have flown a long way. Are you staying locally?"

"Yes. I have a house in Sydney. It belongs to my family and is welcome when we travel here."

"A home from home."

She smiles sweetly. "The best kind there is."

I notice her attention is distracted as she stares at her husband and my heart starts beating rapidly as I wonder if this is the moment I've been waiting for. Then she looks away and attempts to disguise the hatred in her eyes, and it makes me wonder about Serena's mom. That wasn't the look of love in her eyes, and I sense trouble in their marriage because of it.

Serena says loudly, "Mr. Romanov, are you staying in Australia for long?"

It gives me the excuse to stare at her directly, and I mask the lust in my eyes by smiling politely. "Sadly no. I will be returning to America on business in two days, before heading back to Russia at the beginning of next month. My father passed away, and it is customary to enjoy a family meal forty days after his death."

"I'm so sorry to hear that, Mr. Romanov." Mrs. Stoner says with sadness and Serena echoes her condolences. However, I am spared from more small talk when Joseph says suddenly, "Is it hot in here, or is it just me?"

We turn and see him wiping the sweat from his brow with the napkin and Sarah says in surprise, "I was thinking it's a little chilly. Are you okay?"

"Do I look okay?" Stoner yells and Serena says icily, "Perhaps you should take a minute, Joe."

He pulls the collar from his neck and says harshly, "I think there must be something wrong with the food."

"It wouldn't act that fast." Sarah says with a hint of concern as she watches him gasp for air.

"Shut up woman, what are you, an expert now?"

Gleb shakes his head as Stoner stands and clutches the table. "I don't feel too good. Call an ambulance, Sarah."

To her credit, Sarah just nods and leaves the room and I say with pretend concern, "Perhaps you should sit down and take some water. It may help."

I hand him the glass and he clutches his chest and wails, "The pain, oh God, the pain. Please help me." He takes a deep, rasping breath. "I think I'm having a heart attack."

Nobody moves. Not one of us bothers to go to his assistance and merely watch the scene unfold with interest rather than concern.

He glances around the room and as the realization dawns in his eyes, I whisper, "Say hi to the devil for me."

He clutches his chest and takes his last breath before falling forward, headfirst on the table, bashing his face as he falls before slipping to the ground.

As he lies there, Gleb makes the sign of the cross and whispers, "May God have mercy on his soul."

Serena stares in disbelief and then, as her eyes meet mine, she smiles. A beautiful smile that makes my heart beat faster as she whispers, "I doubt God will be involved, Gleb. I expect his soul is heading straight to hell."

CHAPTER 27

SERENA

*A*s I stare at the body on the floor, it's with an inner peace I wasn't expecting. I don't know what just happened, but I'm glad it did.

I don't have time to react because mom returns and stares at the scene with a stunned expression.

"Joe." She gasps as she races to his side and as she crouches down beside him, she feels for a pulse before raising her eyes and saying in a hushed whisper, "He's dead."

I push back from my seat and go to her side, grasping her hand and saying softly, "I'm sorry, mom."

She shakes her head. "I can't believe it. Is this really happening?"

I nod, a little surprised by her reaction but sad for her at the same time.

"It appears he suffered a heart attack, Mrs. Stoner. Please accept my condolences."

Alexei says respectfully and mom shakes her head and whispers, "He really is dead."

Alexei catches my eye and appears as confused as I am and I say gently, "You're in shock. I'll fetch you a drink."

"No!" Mom says firmly and then stands, fixing Stoner with an unreadable expression.

"What happens now?" She says almost to herself, and Alexei says gently, "The ambulance will take charge of his body. They will call the cops if they think it's necessary."

"The cops?"

Mom's eyes widen and I say quickly, "It's standard procedure, mom. I doubt they will discover anything other than it was a heart attack. Knowing his lifestyle, he was probably a ticking bomb, anyway."

"I suppose." Mom stares at me with an expression that makes me think she knows more about this than I thought. She says with an air of dignity, "Please. We should respect my husband. I'll fetch something to cover him with."

I stare down at the lifeless body at our feet, his face purple due to the blood pouring from his broken nose and his eyes wide open in fear. It wasn't the most dignified of passings, and I stare at him with a growing sense of derision. I feel nothing but relief that he's dead. Mom is free and he can't hurt her anymore.

As I glance at Alexei, his eyes flash and something tells me he knows a little about what happened here today and rather than being afraid about that, it only makes me like him more. His warning about the drinks reveals his murder weapon, and I'm impressed how well it was executed.

* * *

THREE HOURS later and the storm subsides. The paramedics arrived and declared Stoner dead. They took his body away and I guess there will be an autopsy. Mom was shocked into silence, and it didn't take much to persuade her to take a bath and try to deal with the shock. Alexei and Gleb remained through it all and dealt with the paramedics on mom's behalf. I'm so grateful they were, providing the calm voice of authority that we really needed.

As mom heads off for her bath, Gleb disappears, leaving me alone with Alexei and as soon as the door closes, I fall into his outstretched arms.

As they fold around me, it's as if I'm home and he buries his face in my hair and whispers, "I came for you, tiger. We have unfinished business."

I pull back and grin. "You made quite the entrance, Mr. Romanov. Do you always murder your business partners after the deal is struck? Is that the Russian way?"

His eyes flash as he whispers huskily, "I don't know what you are talking about."

His wicked grin tells me I'm right and so I lean forward and kiss his lips hard, loving how his hand snakes around the back of my head and grips my hair, holding my head in position as he dominates my mouth.

I am drowning in desire as I press hard against him, because apparently witnessing a murder turns me on. I am in no doubt at all, Alexei caused this, and I've never wanted him anymore than I do now.

It's so frustrating because I want nothing more than to leave with him and carry on where we left off on the aircraft, but mom needs me now and so, as we pull apart, I say huskily, "I want to be with you so badly, Alexei but mom is my priority right now."

He strokes my face and stares deeply into my eyes and whispers, "I'm in Sydney for two more days. I'll send a car for you tomorrow night when your mom is sleeping. Spend the night with me, little one. We have a lot to talk about."

"Talk?" I stare at him with heated lust. "You had better not do much talking, Alexei."

He grins. "Then we are on the same page. Tomorrow night, Serena. I promise you won't regret it."

He pulls away as Gleb enters the room and says with a loud sigh, "I'm sorry to interrupt but there is a police officer asking for you, Serena."

"For me?" I stare at Alexei in confusion, and he takes my hand. "I expect the hospital reported it as a sudden death. It will be routine."

"Okay." I take a deep breath. "You had better show him in."

The officer is obviously uncomfortable as we sit opposite him and report what happened. He writes our statements down and then runs through the facts before saying, "I'm sorry for your loss, Miss Vieri. I am also sorry to ask if your mom is up to giving a statement."

"Of course." I stand. "I'll ask her to join us."

I leave the officer with Alexei and Gleb and hurry to mom's room and as I enter, I find her staring out of the window at the police car below in the courtyard.

"What did you tell him?" She says without looking around and I say softly, "The truth, mom. Just tell him what happened at dinner. They are the facts anyway."

"Is it terrible that I'm glad he's dead, Serena?"

Mom turns and I note the frozen expression on a face devoid of grief.

"No." I shake my head. "I kind of already figured out you couldn't stand the man."

I grin. "That makes two of us."

She smiles sadly. "I keep on replaying the scene in my mind. It fascinated me. Does that make me a bad person, especially as I didn't move to help him?"

"Nobody did, mom. That says a lot about the man he was."

"I suppose you're right."

She takes a deep breath and smiles. "I suppose I should get this over with. I'm glad you're here, Serena. It means a lot."

As she heads toward me, she takes my hand, and we leave the

room together in silence. It's as if when Stoner died, a breath of fresh air brought new life into this house because the atmosphere is not so repressive anymore. There's just a welcome relief knowing we never have to see him again.

CHAPTER 28

ALEXEI

*T*wenty-four hours feels like twenty-four weeks, and I wonder about that. What began as a wild adventure has turned into something I'm still coming to terms with. I don't chase after women. I never have and yet I have an insatiable desire to be always close to Serena and I suppose it's because I've never met anyone quite like her before.

I kept my mind on business, which has always been my main focus, but inside I've been counting down the hours until now.

As I wait for her with a glass of vodka in my hand, I stare across the Sydney skyline and plan my next move.

Life has always been a game of chess for me. Outwitting my opponent is the aim of the game. Now it's securing my latest infatuation by my side until I have tired of her.

Right now, I can't imagine that ever being a possibility, but I'm a realist and realize it's just the chase that interests me. Serena is not my usual conquest, which is why I'm so enamored of her. The thrill will fade when I'm bored with playing and I don't really expect any different.

"Alexei."

Her soft voice reaches me across the darkened room, and I turn slowly and stare at the goddess who has walked into my web.

She dazzles in the same red dress she wore yesterday evening, and those heels are a very welcome sight indeed.

"I'm glad you could make it, despite the unfortunate situation at home." I say with a lazy grin as I drag my eyes the length of her body, salivating at what will soon follow.

"I wouldn't miss this for the world." She grins, her gaze assessing me as I stand before her in nothing but the silk pants I wore on the plane.

She stares at me with a hunger I share, and I say huskily, "You are a little overdressed for what I have in mind."

I watch as she unzips the dress slowly and steps out of it like a butterfly emerging from a chrysalis, wearing nothing but the tattoo I gifted her and a lustful smile.

She walks toward me in the red heels and whispers, "I could say the same about you."

Without breaking eye contact, I lower my pants and step out of them, facing her with a raging hard-on and a wicked glint in my eye. She stops before me and, with a sexy grin, drops to her heels and takes my cock in her hand, her nails scratching my balls as she licks the pre-cum from the head. She swirls her tongue around the top and caresses my balls and I stare down at her in fascination as the lights of the city glisten like stars outside the uncovered window.

I love how fearless she is and how she matches my mood without any questions.

She takes me to the back of her throat, and I groan as my cock slides home where it belongs. Inside any part of this woman will do. She is home to me right now, and I didn't appreciate how much I needed this. Needed *her* and as she sucks my cock and rolls my balls in her gentle fingers, I swear I relax for the first time in ages.

I fist her hair and thrust in hard, using her willing mouth as a receptacle for my desire, pushing in fast and deep as she groans her appreciation as she sucks me hard.

There are no other sounds but the moans of lust as two people carry on where they left off and as the tension builds, I pull out and growl, "Swap with me."

She stands, her ass against the window as I drop to my knees and return the favor. Parting her thighs with a feral growl as I take her clit in my mouth and suck gently, loving how she tastes of honey and sin, which is my newfound addiction. I tease her clit as she moans and as her legs tremble, I pull away and whisper, "Turn around."

As she presses her body to the window, I move behind her and grip her hips, pulling her back against my hard cock as I tease her from behind.

She leans back against me, and I nip at her neck, whispering, "This is what I need."

She pushes back against my cock and whispers, "Stop talking."

It makes me smile as I slide in home, surprised at the rush of emotion I experience when I am fully inside her. She moans, her breath rapid and loaded with desire as I push in deeper, loving the wet trail easing me inside. As I bite her neck, I hold her hips and shove harder inside, dominating my woman, giving her nowhere to go. As I plunge in hard and fast, the sensations overpowering me are of lust and desperation. I needed this—I needed her and one night is nowhere near long enough.

Her scream of ecstasy is accompanied by a wet burst of heat as she milks my cock, causing me to explode inside her, loving how she shudders against me.

I bury my face in her neck and push in deeper, prolonging every second of this amazing sensation. This isn't sex. It's a declaration and as I run my arms around her body, I pull her against me and hold on tight. I still don't know what it is about this woman that intrigues me so much, but I do know I am nowhere near finished with her yet.

She turns and smiles up into my eyes. "I missed you, Alexei."

"Same." I stroke her face lightly and grin. "I was cheated out of more adventures with you."

"I feel the same." She sighs and leans against my chest as my arms fold around her.

"How is your mom?"

I'm touched that she asks, and I say with a heavy heart. "She's just about coping. It's a huge loss to us all, but especially to her."

"It's ironic, really."

She nestles into my arms, and it is so good to be with her again.

"What is?" I kiss the top of her head and she says sadly, "Your mom is devastated, whereas mine is ecstatic."

That surprises me and I pull back and stare at her with interest. "Why?"

She shrugs. "Their marriage, as it turns out, wasn't a happy one, and he was no longer the man she met back in Chicago."

"I see." It would explain a lot and I say evenly.

"We need to talk."

"Talk?" She grins up at me. "I prefer actions rather than words."

I hate to be responsible for tearing that smile from her face, but she deserves to hear the truth.

"Come. We can eat on the terrace. Despite what you believe, I intended to feed you tonight. The table is set overlooking the opera house."

As I take her hand and lead her to the terrace, I grab two robes that I placed nearby earlier. As I help her on with one of them, I kiss her lips softly and whisper, "Only I get to see you naked, Serena. I am very possessive of my things."

"Your things?" She raises her well-defined brow, "I am no

man's *thing*, Mr. Romanov, but I'm open to discussion on the subject and just so you know, I'm a mean negotiator."

I smirk as we head out onto the terrace because I always get what I want and right now, I want Serena Vieri and I will agree to anything to make it happen.

CHAPTER 29

SERENA

I was past the point of no return, and I couldn't deny him if I tried.

From the second I walked into his apartment and saw him standing by the window, I knew what happened soon after was inevitable. I wanted it more than anything, which is why I was so brazen. It was as if I was a paid whore brought in to do a job and I loved the sense of freedom it gave me.

However, I'm kidding myself if I thought that was just sex. Not for me. It meant something. The way my heart raced, and my breathing intensified wasn't because of a physical attraction. It was the man behind the wicked smile who is the object of my fascination and desire. The man I haven't been able to stop thinking about since we met and shared an impossible adventure with.

We step out onto the terrace, and I gasp at the view. Sydney has never looked so beautiful to me and as I gaze down on the harbor and see the opera house illuminated against the skyline, I have never been happier.

I glance at Alexei with a delighted smile, and he returns it with a soft look of pleasure.

"Wow, you impress me every single fucking time, Alexei. This view is amazing."

"It is." He draws me close and stares into my eyes and whispers huskily. "You are the perfect view, Serena, one I've missed."

"You hardly know me to miss me." I say quickly, disguising the fact I am intoxicated by his words. Nobody misses me and nobody stares at me as if I'm the most important person in their world. I feel like that with him. It's as if anything is possible and we could move mountains together.

He kisses me softly and this time more leisurely, as if we have all the time in the world and I wish that was the case. I don't ever want this moment to end, but it inevitably does.

He pulls back and says with a wry smile. "Come. We should eat and I'll tell you a story."

Something in his expression tells me I may not like it and as he pours me a glass of red wine, I prepare myself for the dream to crash and burn.

I say nothing at all as he tells me what happened when they caught up with the flight attendant. Finding out I was the intended target isn't a surprise, but it's still a shock to hear.

"I'm sorry, Serena. At least we discovered it in time." He says with a gentle smile.

"This time." I reply with a shake of my head. "The threat is still hanging over me. Did she tell you who ordered it?"

This is the million-dollar question, and from the look in his eyes, I'm not going to like the answer.

"I'm sorry, Serena. She said it was your aunt, Giselle Matasso."

It's as if he has punched me hard and I am struggling to breathe. For a second I can only stare at him in shock, not really believing I heard him right.

"My aunt?" I say in a low whisper, and he nods, reaching out and grasping my hand in a show of sympathy that touches me.

"But why?" I am stunned, and he says with concern.

"I was hoping you could tell me that."

160

"I can't."

I feel sick and he says softly, "You told me your father ordered a hit on you all and your brother got there first. Is it possible your aunt and father were working together?"

"I suppose."

I still can't believe we are having this discussion at all, and he strokes my hand lightly, which is exactly what I need to keep me focused.

"But what would she gain by killing me? It doesn't make sense."

Alexei smiles ruefully. "I haven't finished my story yet?"

"You mean there's more?" I'm not sure if I can take any more and he says angrily, "She wasn't acting alone."

"Who, and please don't say my grandparents."

I'm not sure I can take any more family members wanting me dead and I stare in fascination as his eyes flash and his lip curls as he spits, "Stoner."

I blink and stare at him in horror.

"Joe Stoner!"

"Yes." Alexei grips my hand a little harder. "They were good friends who go way back. It appears that your aunt wanted to cause trouble in your family and arranged it so your mother discovered your father cheating on her. She encouraged her to leave and offered to put her up in her penthouse in the city where she met Stoner in the elevator one day."

"They planned it. But why?"

I still can't believe it and Alexei carries on, "It worked. She fell in love with him, probably because he was being everything she wanted at the time. It broke up your parents' marriage and took her away from you."

He sighs heavily. "Something must have happened in the past to make your aunt seek revenge. I'm guessing you need to question that and when you find the answer, you will have your reason."

"Thank you." I stare at him with a hardening expression and my emotion turns cold inside me. It was the same when I discovered our father had ordered the hit on us and it will be the same for her. I need to discover their motives if we stand any chance of unraveling this mystery, and there are only two people who can help me with this who I trust with my whole heart.

"I can't deal with this alone, Alexei." I stare at him with determination.

"You're not on your own, tiger. You have your brothers, and you have me."

"You would help me. Why?"

"Because I like a challenge, I suppose." He laughs softly, and it cuts the tension in seconds.

"My life is a constant challenge; you may not be able to keep up." I say drily, and he grips my hand a little tighter.

"I can run and negotiate business at the same time, Serena. The only question is, can you keep up with me?"

"What do you think?" I say with a chuckle, and he nods. "Then we do this together. I will be your back up and help you unravel the mystery and in return…"

"What?" My breath hitches at the desire in his eyes as he growls, "I want you, Serena."

He stares at me hard. "In my bed, by my side and at my beck and call."

"At your beck and call?" I laugh out loud. "Too far, Alexei." I sigh heavily. "Your terms are like you. Arrogant."

I laugh softly. "But I kind of like an arrogant man, so I agree to the first two, but only for as long as I want to be there."

My eyes flash as he leans back and smirks, his robe falling open, revealing that flawless body that could ruin a seasoned nun.

"Then I shall work hard to keep you, Serena."

"Keep me?" I lean forward, my own robe offering him a glimpse of my tits. "I am not a possession, Alexei. I never have been, and I never will be. I'm not my mother and make my own decisions. I will *not* be at your beck and call, but I will be by your side, but only because I want to be."

"Then we have an agreement." He reaches out to shake my hand and, as his rough hand covers mine, I shiver inside. Then I raise my eyes to his and grin. "You're a shit negotiator, Alexei, because I would have agreed for nothing."

He grips my hand hard and says huskily, "And I would have helped you for nothing. Apparently, we both wanted the same thing, anyway."

Despite the fact he just blew my world apart, he pieced it swiftly back together with his next sentence. With him beside me, I could fight wars and I am in no doubt at all this is what this is. This time, however, the blood that spills is family and there is nothing more painful than that.

CHAPTER 30

ALEXEI

*I*t's been two weeks since Joseph Stoner died, and Serena flew home yesterday with her mom. Our contact has been limited because she is dealing with more shit than me right now and I am also preoccupied with family matters.

We learned that my father's heart attack was unexplained. There was no reason physically why he suffered one, and yet there was nothing showing what could have caused it.

Untraceable.

That is the one word that haunts me, and I replay the moment Stoner died in my head a million times. Gleb produced the report of Stoner's death, and it was identical findings, which tells me we have a huge problem.

I relayed the information to my brothers, and we are now investigating the probable cause that our father was murdered. But who by?

It has occupied most of my time and I'm weary of it. There are no answers, and Mikhail is on a mission to discover exactly who is responsible. He is working his way through a list of enemies as if it's a tick list and the rest of us are doing our best to feed him information.

I am caught between two families at war and yet, rather than focus on my own shit, I am more concerned about Serena's. She is not safe all the time her aunt lives, and I hate knowing she isn't by my side where I can protect her.

Tonight, is a charity auction that was arranged by her brother Killian and his wife Purity. They are one of the most powerful couples in society right now and tickets to it are like gold dust. If you are not invited to any of their gatherings, you are considered a nobody and it will be interesting to see who was left off the guest list rather than the ones congratulating themselves they are there at all.

I dress in my customary black dinner jacket and white shirt. My black tie fastened impeccably, and my rare Rolex fastened securely to my wrist. I am in no doubt I am high on that guest list because the Romanovs bleed power wherever they visit. I am in demand socially and tonight was no exception. Knowing that Serena will be there made me eager to go, although she may not approve of my plus one.

"She's here, Alexei." Gleb puts down his phone and shakes his head.

"Are you sure about this?"

"Are you questioning my choices, Gleb?" I glare at him, and he rolls his eyes. "Yes. Of course I am. Miss Vieri may not enjoy seeing you with another woman hanging off your arm.'

"I'm counting on it, Gleb."

He shakes his head. "I'll never understand you, Alexei."

"Then I am pleased to hear that, Gleb, because the moment you do, I have failed."

He rolls his eyes once again, which makes me smile. Sparring with Gleb amuses me and I secretly love that he calls me out on my shit with no regard for my position.

We glance up as the elevator door opens and Regina heads

into the room, in a black dress with a split that runs up to her thigh. She walks on the highest heels and her hair is piled high on top of her head, diamonds sparkling at her throat and her eyes shining as brightly with excitement.

"Alexei." She nods to Gleb.

"Gleb. It's good to see you again."

She stares at me with interest.

"I was surprised to receive your invitation."

"Good." I shrug. "I'm guessing not many things in life surprise you, Regina."

"It was a pleasant one."

Her eyes flash with an invitation that is as clear as she is standing before me, and I turn and pour three glasses of champagne into three glasses.

"We should toast a successful mission."

I hand one to each of them and raise my glass.

"To a satisfactory business partnership."

Gleb hates every minute of this, and his disapproval is written all over his face as he watches Regina direct a smoldering glance in my direction. He has witnessed many meetings like this and knows they end with my companion being fucked senseless before being sent home in the early hours, and he will think this is no different. Regina obviously thinks so too, because the lust in her eyes is focused solely on me as I stare at her with a deepening gaze.

We finish our drinks in silence, and I nod toward the elevator. "Our car is waiting. Shall we?"

Regina nods, her chest heaving and an excited flush to her cheeks as I take her hand and guide her toward the elevator. Outwardly, I am the perfect host, but inside I am burning with revenge. Regina is my key to unlocking this mystery, and I will use her for information. She doesn't know it yet, but she has been invited here for a very good reason and it will be interesting to see if I was right.

* * *

THE EXCELSIOR HOTEL is the venue for the charity gala, and the paparazzi are out in their entirety tonight. As our limo stops by the red carpet, we exit the car and take our positions in front of the giant backdrop advertising the event. I'm aware our photographs will be immediately posted online with various reporters casting their opinion on our presence.

Regina looks stunning next to me, holding onto my arm as we pose for the photographs required for this evening. Killian is determined to raise awareness for the charity and solidify his position as the most generous benefactor in society.

She is loving the attention, which surprises me because assassins usually prefer to remain hidden in the shadows. She is an exception to that as she stands in full sight and dazzles, relying on the fact nobody would suspect a sweet innocent woman who is one of them.

Her occupation affords her the perfect cover, and she definitely doesn't do it for the money they pay. She does it to pass through airports undetected and leave before anyone even suspects she was involved.

As we walk into the main reception, she whispers with excitement. "Thank you for inviting me, Alexei. I just want to say I don't hold what happened when we last met against you. I know it was only business, so I'm grateful for the opportunity to make it up to you."

It amuses me because she is completely unaware that I'm using her for information, but I just smile. "Business is one thing, but pleasure is a different one entirely."

I note the hope flare in her eyes as she rewards me with a seductive smile, and it irritates me that these women are so easily manipulated. She would forgive a threat to her life in the hope of ending up beneath me later tonight. It reminds me that I am so done with these vultures and casually glance around the room in the hope of seeing the one person I am aching to be around.

She will be pissed, I already know that, but business always comes first, and my business is protecting her whether she approves of my methods or not.

CHAPTER 31

SERENA

*M*om is quiet beside me as we travel in the third car toward the event.

"Are you okay, mom?" I ask, placing my hand on her arm in a gesture of support.

"It's strange being back here." She says sadly. "It's as if Australia was another life. There are so many memories surrounding me here, and most of them are bad ones."

It hurts me knowing mom is suffering and I don't really blame her. She accompanied me back here for a visit, so she wasn't left alone to deal with the shit Stoner's death caused.

His death was ruled as natural causes. A heart attack brought on by excessive living. He was buried and aside from me and my mother, the rest of the mourners were business associates and staff. Mom kept her delight in his passing well-hidden and played the grieving widow in public, but was more like her old self in private.

We discussed her future, and she decided she would rather move back home and find a house somewhere exclusive and enjoy her life as a single woman for once. She doesn't want to be part of our world anymore and we are welcome to use her home as an escape from it. I fully understand that and am helping her choose the perfect place, although she has her sights set on Los Angeles because she is now accustomed to a hotter climate.

"Do we have to stay long?" She says with a sigh, and I reply sharply, "This is Killian's evening. We will stay as long as he wants us to."

She smiles. "You are so loyal, Serena. You always put family first. You are a true Vieri."

"Of course." I shrug. "It will always be that way."

For some reason, her words anger me because she was a Vieri once. She knows how it works, but my argument is no longer valid given the example of my own father and now my aunt.

The car stops at the red carpet and mom exhales sharply. "Let's get this over with."

I am helped from the car by Connor, who I still haven't apologized to enough for deserting him at the airport. He is a true loyal soldier though and carries on as we did before, but I still feel bad about the shit he suffered as a result of letting me slip through the net.

It's only because I pleaded with my grandfather to reinstate him as my bodyguard that he is here at all and I know I have a lot to do to make it up to him because despite acting as if he has a stick up his ass most of the time, he is loyal to me and probably always will be.

We pose for photographs and then head inside, and mom says petulantly, "I hate these things. I haven't missed them at all."

I choose to ignore her comment because she is seriously pissing me off now and I will be happy when she is settled into her own home, and I can go back to being her daughter from afar. It strikes me that mom was always irritating. Always complaining and being critical of our lifestyle. My brothers escape it most of the time and I truly believe she is a little scared of them. I am the one who bears the brunt of her disillusionment, and it can be hard to endure after a while.

As we move through the crowd, my guards keep a respectful distance, scanning the room for threats and keeping strangers away from us.

We help ourselves to two glasses of champagne and as my mom smiles her thanks, it strikes me how alike we are. She is the beauty in the Vieri family with her sleek black hair and flashing blue eyes. She has taken good care of herself and I don't miss the attention she attracts as we move through the room. My father always did like the best, and my mom was the beauty most men wanted by their side. That's why her marriage to Stoner was so surprising, and it was even more surprising that she allowed him to control her.

I see Shade and Allegra standing in the circle of his own dark menace and as the guards part, the couple breaks apart and I grin at the flush on Allegra's face as she sees who is joining them.

Shade is as arrogant as usual, and it doesn't take a genius to work out he was doing something inappropriate before we came.

"Shade, honey." Mom kisses him on both cheeks and then turns to his girlfriend. "You must be, Allegra. I have been dying to meet you."

"Mrs. Stoner." Allegra stares at mom with wide eyes and I can tell she is intimidated.

"Call me Sarah, please." Mom smiles and I catch Shade's eye, noting the usual irritation in his.

"We must have lunch together." Mom says to Allegra, who nods vigorously. "I would love that. Thank you."

Shade leans against the wall and raises Allegra's hands to his lips and smiles in his usual lazy way. "Have you seen Killian yet?" he asks, and I shake my head. "We just got here."

He points to an opening in the crowd where I watch Purity laughing at something as my brother glowers beside her. They are talking to a well-known actor and his date, and the rage in Killian's eye is almost palpable.

Shade grins. "I love watching him trying to keep his shit together. It's so entertaining."

"Is that his wife?" Mom says as she stares in awe at Purity, who dazzles like an angel beside our arrogant brother.

"Yes, but good luck getting a minute alone with her." Shade drawls, "Killian's name has replaced overprotective in the dictionary."

It makes me grin, but that soon fades when I see who has just walked in.

It's as if my heart is ripped out while I'm still breathing and flung into the pit of hell when I see a beautiful woman gazing adoringly into Alexei's eyes. It's as if my world stops spinning and everyone around me fades into a blur as I stare at the man I gave my heart to, tossing it back at me, ripped and bloodied at my feet.

"Well, that's interesting." Shade drawls as we watch them head across to us, giving me nowhere to run. I have no time to hide as they arrive in our inner circle and for some reason, it's not me Alexei is staring at.

I can only stare at the woman holding onto his arm and if I had a gun right now, I would empty it between her eyes. I am barely conscious of the introductions, but even in my shocked state, I notice something is happening I should really be aware of.

CHAPTER 32

ALEXEI

*A*s soon as I saw her standing there, my heart died a thousand deaths. The pain in her eyes hit me hard across the room and the devastation on her face was quickly concealed by a mask of pure rage. My heart sinks knowing I destroyed the one woman I am trying to protect by using the one who tried to take her from me.

We head across the room and yet it's not for Serena's benefit that I staged this introduction.

As we approach, my eyes are on only one woman and her reaction confirms I was right.

Sarah Stoner is staring at Regina as if she has seen a ghost and yet Regina hasn't even faltered. She is staring around the group as if they are strangers and yet Sarah appears to wish she was somewhere else entirely. She must sense my scrutiny because she glances up and as our eyes meet, I can tell she understands. The fear I register in her eyes confirms my suspicions, which makes my next introduction even more interesting.

Shade is watching the scene with enjoyment and as I greet him, he smiles in his usual lazy way. "Alexei. We meet again. Please introduce us to your guest."

I can't even look at Serena, but I can feel her pain. It almost brings me to my knees, but I steadfastly ignore her and remember who I am and face the group with cold indifference.

"Please allow me to introduce Regina Silver."

Serena stares at her with a sharp look of distaste as Regina positively glows beside me.

"I'm pleased to meet you all."

It leaves Shade's girlfriend to break the awkward silence as she says pleasantly, "Hi, I'm Allegra and this is Shade."

Regina nods. "We have met before. How are you, Shade?"

I can sense Allegra's surprise and note the way Shade grips her hand hard and grins at Regina. "It's been a long time. Are you still flying around the world pretending to work?"

"Of course." Regina smiles and turns her attention to Serena. "Miss Vieri. I've heard so much about you."

"And I you, Miss Silver, none of it flattering."

Regina stiffens as Serena says darkly, "Now, if you'll excuse me, I should mingle."

She pushes her way out of the circle and her mom says quickly, "I should go with her... um..." She can't even look at Regina as she says, "Have a good evening, everyone."

As they leave, it takes all my willpower not to run after them, and Shade grins. "Please excuse my sister, Regina. She doesn't react kindly to social conversation with the person who was hired to murder her."

"Shade!" Allegra's eyes are wide and I'm almost amused when Regina falters and says quickly, "I'm sorry, I don't know what you're talking about."

Shade laughs out loud. "Just walk away, Regina, before you can't."

I pull her from the circle a lot more frightened than when she entered it and she whispers, "They know. Fuck you, Alexei, what's going on?"

I say nothing as my next target is now talking to our hosts

and so with grim determination, I pull her reluctantly toward them. When she sees where we're heading, she tries to pull away and I force her into my arms and, leaning down, growl, "Trust me, Regina. This is for my benefit, not yours, and you have nothing to fear. Play your part and then Gleb will make certain you are escorted home safely. Nobody is concerned about you; you are merely here for information purposes."

"Why?" She is shaking and I suppose I would be in her position. She is surrounded by more evil than one of the Devil's welcome parties in hell and so I reassure her. "Just play along and I will make sure you are safe. Keep your cool and act as if you are any normal date on my arm."

"Okay." She smiles up at me and I'm guessing to anybody looking on, we are close for a very different reason entirely and I hope to God Serena isn't seeing this.

I make a show of touching her face with my hand and staring into her eyes, mainly to diffuse the situation building because I need Regina to be relaxed for my next introduction.

It has the desired effect, and she whispers, "Leave with me, Alexei. We can have a party of our own."

I say nothing and, gripping her hand, I turn and pull her toward the next test.

I note Killian's sharp gaze as we enter the group and his wife stares at us with a beautiful smile as Killian says gruffly, "Alexei, it's good to see you again. This is my wife Purity and my aunt, Giselle."

I nod as Regina shakes beside me and Purity stares at her with concern before smiling sweetly.

"I'm Purity." She holds out her hand, and Regina shakes it politely. "Regina. I'm pleased to meet you."

Killian gazes at her with a blank expression and says gruffly, "Regina. I am a fan of your work, but often find your decisions a little misguided."

Regina obviously wishes she was anywhere else but here and

says nervously, "I understand. I'll make sure my future decisions would meet with your approval."

I stare at Giselle, who appears bored already and as she meets my eye, she says politely, "Mr. Romanov. I have heard of you; my husband Carlos spoke of your father warmly. I was sorry to hear about his untimely death."

I nod. "Thank you, Mrs. Matasso. I will pass your condolences on to my mother."

"How is she? It's been years since I saw her last?"

If anything, she appears to be asking about an old friend and I wonder if she knows my mother learned of her past. If anything, her expression is one of polite conversation, not to dig for information, so I just nod respectfully. "She is coping and is surrounded by her family. Thank you for asking."

Regina is quiet beside me and probably wishes she was anywhere but here and as I see a flash of red disappear out of the reception area, I know my work here is done.

"It was good to see you again, Killian. I won't take up any more of your time."

He nods but I catch the expression in his eye telling me our conversation will be revisited in a more private setting. Both Shade and Killian are aware of my interest in their family and this stunt was also for their benefit, which is why Regina is still breathing after apparently seeking to murder their sister.

We head over to Gleb, and I say dismissively, "Make sure Regina gets home safely. Our work here is done."

She stares at me in disappointment.

"You're not coming?"

"No, Regina. This was not a date; it was a business transaction. You may now leave."

Her eyes glisten with a mixture of tears and anger and she is wise to say nothing at all and follow Gleb from the room. As I watch her go, there is an ache in my heart because my little stunt may have cost me a lot more than I am willing to pay.

CHAPTER 33

SERENA

J had to get away. That was too cruel. Why did Alexei bring that woman here, of all places? He must have done it to upset me, but I don't know why.

Surely, he realized that even seeing him with another woman would wound me deeply, and yet he did it, anyway.

Mom is silent beside me as we head to the restroom and as soon as the door closes, she says wearily. "That was intense."

"What was?" I play it cool, and she stares at me with concern. "It appears that Mr. Romanov is playing a game."

"I wouldn't know?" I shrug, reapplying my lipstick as if I couldn't give a fuck what Alexei does with his time.

"That woman."

"His date." I hate even saying the word and mom nods. "There was something I didn't like about her."

There is an awful lot I don't like about her, mainly that she was sent to kill me, but I say nothing and attempt a smile.

"She means nothing, mom. She *is* nothing, so I suggest you forget about her. Women like that don't last long in our world, and I doubt you will ever see her again."

"Sarah."

We glance up as the restroom door opens and my heart falls when I see my aunt enter.

"Giselle." Mom kisses her three times and smiles.

"You're looking well."

My aunt shrugs. "It comes with being a widow. I'm sure you will soon feel the same effects. I'm sorry for your loss. Joe was a good man."

Mom nods, rewarding her with a shaky smile.

"He was the best. We were so happy."

I stare at her in surprise because it's as if she wants everyone to believe they were deeply in love, and I note the flicker of rage that lights in my aunt's eyes and wonder if there's something I'm missing.

Mom shakes her head. "I came back with Serena to start again. I'm thinking of buying a house to be near my children. I've missed them so much."

She tries to disguise it, but I note the irritation in my aunt's eyes, and I can sense the tension between the two women. It's as if they are playing a game that I don't know the rules of and every sentence they speak has another meaning entirely. It's almost in code and I am fascinated to watch the events unfold.

"Then I wish you luck, Sarah."

My aunt says with an insincere smile. "Now, if you'll excuse me, I should really address the reason I came in here for."

As my aunt heads into the cubicle, I notice the triumphant gleam in my mom's eyes before she replaces it with a soft look directed at me.

"Come. We should mingle. There are many people I need to catch up with. It's been so long."

As we leave the restroom and head into the reception room, I try desperately hard *not* to search for Alexei in the crowd. I really don't want to watch him with another woman because it hurts too much and I wish I could just slip away and head home for an early night instead, alone with my misery.

As we make our way through the crowd, mom is stopped by a family friend and as they chat, Gleb appears by my side.

"Good evening, Serena. You are looking particularly lovely tonight."

"Thanks." I smile at him warmly because I really like Alexei's assistant and then he leans closer and whispers, "Alexei has asked if you'll join him on the terrace."

"I think you've asked the wrong woman, Gleb. Perhaps he meant the woman who tried to kill me."

Gleb shakes his head. "Listen to him, Serena. Nothing is ever what it seems."

I hate that I'm intrigued and know in my heart I should be running as soon as he calls but I am interested in hearing his excuse, so I nod.

"He has two minutes."

Gleb nods respectfully and as we move toward the terrace, I note Connor as usual, keeping a discreet distance behind me, watching my back as he always has done.

I head outside and immediately see Alexei leaning against the balustrade, watching me. The moon shines behind him along with the stars, and yet the only thing I can focus on is the man I approach with an angry glare.

"You've got a nerve asking me to meet you, Mr. Romanov." I say in an icy voice as I approach and his eyes gleam as he whispers huskily, "A wise woman would maintain silence until she knows all the facts."

"A wise woman wouldn't be here at all, Mr. Romanov, so now we both know I am not wise, merely angry, perhaps you will do me the honor of telling me what the fuck that was all about?"

I note the fire in his eyes as he reaches out and pulls me against him, tipping my face to his and whispering, "I have answers and you need to listen."

"To what?" I brush my lips against his and am delirious with desire, despite my anger toward him.

"It appears that your aunt isn't the only family member playing the game."

I pull back and stare at him with concern.

"What are you talking about?"

He silences me by placing his finger on my lips and says huskily, "Not here. Tonight, you will accompany me home and stay the night."

"In your dreams, asshole."

I bite back, and he shakes his head. "Non-negotiable, even if I have to kidnap you."

"I'd like to see you try."

I nod toward my bodyguard, who is glowering in the corner and Alexei grins.

"One man isn't an army, Serena. He can come too, by the way."

"Why would I want that?"

I laugh softly because I just can't help being so happy I'm back in his arms.

"Make your excuses and leave with me. Tell your brothers but nobody else."

"Why them?" I'm confused and he whispers, "Because they realize the safest place for you is by my side tonight."

"Will you just tell me what's going on, Alexei, because I'm pissed now. Why do my brothers know something I don't?"

"Because my date tonight was for their information. I told them of my plans, and they have approved them."

I pull back and stare at him with anger and hiss, "Then fuck you, Alexei, because if you are talking to my brothers behind my back, we have nothing more to say."

I am so enraged I can't see straight because what the actual hell? Why am I always the last to know? The men who surround me think they have the right to dictate my life and cut me out of discussions. I thought Alexei was better than that. It appears I was wrong.

I make to turn away and he grips me hard and whispers, "You have twenty minutes to say your goodbyes. My car will be waiting for you and if you aren't in it, I'll be coming for you personally. Oh, there is another reason you need to be in that car."

"What reason?" I hitch my breath as he grazes his lips against mine and whispers, "We still have several hours of an adventure left to enjoy. Don't back out on me now, tiger."

I break away before I say something I'll regret and head back to the reception. I have twenty minutes to get the answers I need before leaving with the man I can't break my addiction for. The trouble is, I couldn't stay if I tried because, like it or not, Alexei Romanov has gotten under my skin and become an itch that needs constant scratching.

CHAPTER 34

ALEXEI

*T*wenty minutes later and I am waiting in my car, glancing at my watch, hoping that Serena doesn't make this difficult for me. Twenty-five minutes pass and I make to leave the car and notice her running down the stairs like fucking Cinderella.

"Sorry." She says, her breath racing. "I was stopped by an over eager friend of my brothers."

"I say nothing and pull her into the car after me and as the door slams, it wastes no time in moving away from the curb.

"So, Alexei..." She doesn't get the chance to finish her sentence as I pull her into my arms and kiss her as if my life depends on it.

If I had any concerns that she was angry with me, I'm reassured as she eases the jacket off my shoulders and pushes her hands under my shirt, raking her nails down my chest and saying huskily, "I fucking hate you right now."

I push her dress up around her waist and pull her panties aside, plunging two fingers deep inside her and whisper, "How much do you hate me now?"

"I detest you." She growls as she bites my lip and cups my balls through the fabric of my pants.

As she unzips them with speed I growl, "What about now?"

"I'm liable to kill you." She groans as I pump three fingers inside her and massage her clit at the same time.

Then she squeezes my cock hard and pumps it furiously, hissing, "I hate you more than anyone in the world right now."

"Why does that turn me on?" I groan as I pull her onto my lap and thrust up inside her hard.

She grips my hair and squeezes my cock, moaning with pleasure as she rides me hard and fast. I thrust up relentlessly and without care and she gasps, "Fuck, Alexei. I hate you so much."

"I'm sure you do, tiger."

I grunt as I press hard on her clit, causing her to tense and then gasp as her entire body convulses on me. I shoot hard inside her, and she leans down and kisses me so fiercely it does something to my heart. I wrap my arms around her and hold on tight as I kiss her with a passion I have never felt before. Her fingers tangle in my hair and I grip hers tightly, holding her head in place as I taste the woman I can't stop thinking about.

When she is not with me, I'm picturing moments like this, desperate for the next fix, because I already know I am addicted to her. I haven't had nearly enough of her yet and tonight I am overdosing on Serena Vieri, even if it kills me.

* * *

THE CAR STOPS ABRUPTLY, causing her to fall back and then against me harder and we hear an apologetic, "Sorry boss, a cat ran into the road." through the privacy screen.

Serena stares at me and then giggles so adorably, I tighten my hold. I am still deep inside her and in no hurry to leave and as she grips me tightly, she lays her head on my shoulder and whispers, "It hurt so much."

She doesn't even need to tell me what she is referring to and I whisper, "It was business. She was there for information purposes only."

"Are you going to tell me?"

She holds me tighter, and I nuzzle her hair and whisper, "Of course."

I reach inside my pocket and pull out a handkerchief and hand it to her as we attempt to disentangle from one another.

She pulls her dress down and sits beside me and as soon as we are respectable, I grasp her hand firmly.

"You're not going to like this, little one."

"Tell me something new." She shakes her head and laughs. "There's not a lot in my life I like, Alexei, unless it involves doing unspeakable things with you."

It makes me laugh. "Then allow me to make your dreams come true."

I grip her hand hard, and she turns, a steely glint in her eyes as she says firmly.

"Regina. What's the story there?"

"I don't believe your aunt and Stoner ordered the hit on you."

"But…" She stares at me in shock.

"My brother Valentin can hack into people's systems, and he used his talents on Regina. He accessed her records and files along with her emails and discovered the thread that concerned you. She uses an email address on the dark web and it's where most of her business comes from and the IP address that the customer used was traced to Australia."

"I don't understand."

She looks so worried I want to shield her from the harsh realities, and I say gently, "If it helps, I don't believe you were in any danger."

"What makes you say that?"

"I suspect Regina was employed by your mom."

"NO!" Serena is devastated and her lower lip trembles and I

reassure her quickly, "Regina was told to drug the martini cocktail on the understanding it was your drink. It was a drug that causes a heart attack in the victim and is untraceable in an autopsy. I watched what happened, knowing that Regina had drugged the cocktail, but everyone but Stoner had champagne. I noticed your mom staring at Stoner as if she was waiting for something. She was anxious, and I knew something wasn't right."

"But Stoner always drank martini cocktails. I can't stand them, and neither can mom."

Serena shakes her head in disbelief. "But why pretend the hit was on me? It doesn't make sense."

"It makes perfect sense." I laugh softly.

"It appears that your mom wanted Stoner dead, and she framed your Aunt Giselle for his murder, should anyone find out. She made certain she wouldn't be blamed if there was an investigation. If anything went wrong, your family would seek revenge against your aunt and Stoner because Regina believed it came from Giselle Matasso and that is why I brought her tonight. I wanted to witness your mom's reaction to her as well as Giselle's. Your mom was unsettled by her presence and your aunt didn't react at all. That told me I was right. Your mom murdered Stoner to set herself free."

Serena leans back and exhales sharply. "Way to go, mom."

She laughs softly. "Well, it worked. So at least she got her wish. I suppose she did learn a few tricks all the time she was married to my father."

"It appears so."

The car stops and I grip Serena's hand tightly.

"We can finally relax. You are safe, your mom is free, and Stoner is where he belongs."

"Well, that's a relief." She turns and leans toward me and kisses me softly on the lips, whispering, "Thank you. It means a lot."

The door opens and I exit the car, pulling her along with me, glad we can finally put this behind us.

This is where we began, nothing but dark desire and some time to kill and I am going to make this a night she will never forget.

CHAPTER 35

SERENA

*I*t's as a heavy load has shifted from my soul. I didn't appreciate how much it was dragging me down until Alexei solved the mystery.

If anything, I'm proud of my mom for taking matters into her own hand and Stoner deserved everything coming to him. That's what happens when you manipulate others to suit your own agenda. You run the risk that they will do the same. He underestimated my mom, and that was his fatal mistake.

Now I'm back where I started. Beside a man who makes my heart race and my senses scramble. A man I can't stop thinking about and desire to be with at all times. He is the first man who has affected me this way, and I suspect it's because I have lived among men like him. Powerful, self-assured and take no shit.

It helps that he's also incredibly handsome with that rugged edge that drives the woman in me to distraction. His sharp suits and heady aftershave are a turn on, but it's those glittering eyes and wicked smile that get me every time. Yes, Alexei Romanov was crafted from the wish list written in my soul, which is probably why it hurt so much seeing him with someone else.

We head up to his penthouse and, much like the one overlooking Sydney harbor, this one surveys the skyline of Chicago in one of the most expensive districts. Like everything about the Romanovs, this penthouse is amazing. It's modern, chic and expensive. I am almost afraid to move out of fear of disturbing the carefully placed objects and stunning décor. Nothing looks used and I stare in wonder at a room that ticks every box I own.

"You really must give me the name of your designer. Your homes are incredible." I say in awe.

"Ask mom, she arranges that shit." Alexei shrugs and tosses his jacket onto the white sofa and kicks off his shoes.

He lifts a remote and the fire in the huge media wall springs to life and soft music plays through hidden speakers. He moves around the room and lights candles and it makes me smile.

"It appears you are setting the scene, Alexei. You're a little presumptuous."

"I like candles. What's the problem?" He grins and drops me a wink that makes my toes curl. There is nothing I don't like about this man, and I really hope the feeling is mutual because I'm not a fool. I know his attention will be fleeting. He told me himself he thrives on adventure and playing the game. He will take what he wants from me and toss me aside before moving onto the next sure thing. I'm guessing most women are sure things around a man like him, and that makes me a little anxious.

I hate how weak he makes me and so I distract my attention away from him and move around the room, taking in the décor and appreciating every designer touch.

"I brought you here for a reason, Serena."

I turn at the tone of his voice because it's unusually business-like. I'm used to the seduction in it but not this harder approach.

I turn and note the hard glint in his eye and for some reason, it makes me nervous.

"Why did you bring me here?" I say slowly and guarded, a slight shiver passing through my body as I sense the atmosphere changing.

He nods toward the couch and says firmly, "You may be better off sitting down."

I say nothing and move across the room because this isn't what I thought we'd be doing now, and as I perch on the edge, my mind is racing into overdrive.

He sits beside me and takes my hand, staring at me with a hard gleam in his eye. It's impossible to read and I sense I'm about to hear something I may wish was never said.

"I believe my father was murdered."

"How?"

I keep to the facts because men like Alexei don't appreciate emotion and he says bitterly, "When I witnessed Stoner's death, it hit me. I pictured my father in his place because what happened was exactly as my mother described. All was well until he had eaten and then complained about the food. Not long after, he was dead."

He squeezes my hand and sighs. "My brothers are of the same opinion as me. Our father was healthy and had regular check-ups and was under no medication. There was no reason for him to suffer a heart attack, and the tests we had run on the body confirmed that."

"I'm so sorry, Alexei." I shake my head. "Do you have any idea who was responsible?"

"No." He growls angrily. "But we will find out and deal with them accordingly."

His voice sends shivers down my spine because I'm under no illusion that whoever did this is a dead man, or woman, walking.

Alexei hisses, "My brother Mikhail is working on it. The tests came back that there was nothing to cause a heart attack. His heart was healthy, and there were no underlying conditions. It just appeared to stop, causing a massive coronary. There was no trace of narcotics or poison, but there was a high level of Aconitine, which is a toxin. It is most noted as a heart poison but is also a potent nerve poison. Raw aconite plants are very poisonous.

They are used as herbs only after processing by boiling or steaming to reduce their toxicity."

"So, you believe his food was laced with these herbs, so it must have been one of your chefs."

I say carefully and his eyes flash as he adds, "The chef was found dead a few days later. He was discovered with a bullet in his brain, and it had nothing to do with the Romanovs."

"I don't understand." I'm shocked, even though stories like this are far from uncommon in my life.

"He was executed, which tells me he knew something that, under interrogation, would help our investigation. Somebody used him to murder our father and my family will stop at nothing to discover their identity and make them pay."

I stare into his flashing eyes and say with determination. "Then we will help. I'll speak to my grandfather. He has contacts. He will use them to gather information."

His eyes soften and he whispers, "Thank you, but you have your own problems to deal with. Sadly, tales like mine are more common than happy ones in our lives, and yours is no exception. No, the reason I'm telling you this is not to enlist your help. It's to offer you a proposition."

"Go on then." I'm intrigued as the shadows are chased away in his eyes and replaced by a strange yearning that captivates me. It appears that Alexei Romanov is a man of deep emotion that doesn't get seen very often and I stare at him in fascination as he holds my hand gently and whispers, "I want to continue our wild adventure past the twenty-three hours we agreed on. I would like to show you the world, little one—*my* world and see where it takes us."

I'm stunned, and he caresses the back of my hand with his thumb and says huskily, "Twenty-three hours is barely a fraction of the time I want to spend with you. I haven't even scratched the surface of what I want us to experience and for a man who has never felt this way before, I'm struggling."

"With what?"

My eyes are wide as I stare at him with a mixture of happiness, shock, and desperation.

"With the idea that you will walk away from me, and this will be over."

"And if I agree?" I keep my voice steady, but inside my emotions are out of control as every word he speaks is aimed straight at my heart that races as he continues.

"We will travel together. I'm a very busy man, little one. I am rarely in the same place for longer than a week and then I'm onto the next business deal. I have never known any different, and it didn't matter before now, but I want you to come with me, to share my life and experience things only I can give you outside of the protection of your family."

"You want me to leave my family? My protection and my future for a wild adventure with you?"

My eyes are wide and disbelieving as I contemplate the storm that would cause in my family. Vieris don't leave the fold. They remain protected and part of the organization. There is no freedom in our lives, just existing for the sake of the society my grandfather created.

"What you are asking is impossible." I say, feeling as if my heart is being crushed inside me. "My grandfather would never allow me to leave. Just the fact I was the target of an assassination not so long ago will make him even more overprotective. He will never allow it."

Alexei's eyes flash and he grips my hand hard and says roughly, "Then stand up to him, Serena. Remember who you are. You are part of him, and you deserve to fight for your future. If that is what you want?"

Once again, the yearning burns in his eyes and I imagine him walking away from me, getting on his plane and flying away forever. I am in no doubt that will happen. He would accept defeat and his pride prevent him from crossing my path again. It appears that it's all or nothing with Alexei Romanov and his proposition is so tempting, I can't think past my deep yearning to say yes. I want to accept. I want to see where this leads for us and he is offering me a freedom I never expected would be mine to grasp with both of my eager hands.

But Alexei doesn't know my grandfather like I do. My brothers would never agree, either. I am the protected mafia princess and that will probably never change, so I paste a bright smile on my face and hide my desperation and whisper, "I will see what I can do, Alexei. Give me twenty-four hours to convince my family. I will try my best because I have never wanted anything more than I want you."

The spark of happiness that lights his eyes is the lit fuse blowing my world apart. I already know they will never agree but he doesn't need to know that now. I am here and for one night only I am going to enjoy my freedom and overdose on Alexei Romanov because it appears that this is all we will have. One night to stoke a lifetime of memories and I must make this count.

CHAPTER 36

ALEXEI

I don't do emotion, not really. The only time was when my father died. Now I'm feeling a strange one as I lay my heart on the line before the woman who has crept in and stolen it. I'm not kidding. I do want her to leave with me. To be the first thing I see when I open my eyes. To protect her, make her happy and enjoy my fucked-up life with her by my side.

We have known one another for such a short period of time I'm not sure how I feel about her. I know I can't let her go, which is a first for me, and I'm a man who always gets what he wants. She is a tricky one though, because she doesn't have the ability to make her own decisions. She is like me in that respect. We are part of an organization that keeps its prisoners tightly locked up with no chance of freedom. I'm prepared to agree to anything to be the one to unlock her cage and let her fly into mine instead.

Twenty-four hours may not be long enough, but I must trust that she will do everything in her power to persuade her family. If she wants it of course. There is still that possibility and so I need to make this evening count.

I tilt her face and pull her lips toward mine, loving the burst of heat inside me as our lips connect and I taste the woman I'm addicted to.

I kiss her gently, but it is loaded with passion because, for the first time in my life, this simple act counts for something incredible.

As the fire flickers in the grate, I unzip her dress slowly and carefully, my fingers brushing against her delicate skin, loving how she shivers under my touch.

We stare at one another in silence, the connection between us strong, more powerful now because there are feelings involved. Her eyes are wide and the soulful expression in them mesmerizes me. Her long black hair glides through my fingers and is luxurious to the touch. I cup her face and she leans into my hand, her eyes flashing with a beauty that brings me under her spell.

I have an insatiable need to own her soul. For her to stare into my eyes and only see me. To be her world and make it a better one. Making her happy will give me a reason to exist.

I ease her down on the couch and say huskily, "Wait just one second."

As she lies back against the soft cushions, her eyes glitter like dark pools of sin, laden with lust and emotion that I rarely get to experience.

I tear off my clothes with a slow deliberation, our eyes connected as if by a magnetic force.

The power between us is palpable as we appear to be on the same page. Nothing matters but what happens now and as I tower above her and stare deep into her eyes, words are no longer necessary.

She runs her hands against my skin and stares at me deeply, a small smile on her lips as she drags her nails against the ink on my skin. She caresses the tiger that sits above my heart, a fresh scar on a body that lives for the pain. She leans forward and presses her lips to the image, and it sends a surge of longing through my entire body. It's as if she can control me just from actions alone and for once in my life, I'm happy to allow it.

I stare into her eyes as I run my hand under her ass and lift it closer, positioning myself between her legs, my cock dancing at the entrance to paradise.

She whispers my name and hearing it on her breath is the sweetest sound as I push inside, slowly, savoring every inch of the flesh I pass through, loving how she is gripping my cock with an ownership I'm happy to accept.

Her eyes glitter as I move harder, deeper and with more power, tearing through her body as I remind it who belongs there.

She arches toward me, and her soft gasp makes me swell even further inside her and I grip her face and force her to keep her eyes on me because as I move inside her body, I am making a statement. She is mine and nothing can change the path we are heading along.

I grip her ass hard, pulling her in deeper. My balls dancing against her sodden entrance and her clit dragging against my shaft. It's almost eerie as the only sounds in the room are made by our bodies, making their own sweet music together, which is the best kind there is.

She trembles under me as I push in and out, increasing the pace and loving her sweet soft moans as her body delights in mine. Her face is flushed and her eyes bright as I explore every inch of her inside. I cup her face with my hand and kiss her lips softly, loving how sweet she tastes as I set up home inside her. It's as if my cock has no other place it would rather be as it takes its time and doesn't rush something that has been building for weeks.

Here, in my family penthouse in her hometown, is where I will claim Serena Vieri as my woman. Stolen from under her family's noses and brought in line to walk by my side. I was lying

STELLA ANDREWS

when I told her she had a choice. She doesn't because if she decides to walk away from me, I have Plan B already prepared.

I am a man of business and have already drawn up the contract. If Serena decides she will not come willingly, then her grandfather will be presented with an offer he would be a fool to refuse. Either way, I am not leaving Serena behind when my jet takes off and she will soon learn that Alexei Romanov doesn't take no for an answer.

"Alexei." Her soft gasp tells me she's close and I whisper, "Come for me, little one, don't hold back."

I stare in awe as she explodes inside, loving her heightened color and the way her eyes roll back in her head. This is the most amazing wonder I have ever seen. She is beautiful all the time, but now she is incandescent. I have never met a woman so powerful, so beautiful, and it's as if God made her purely to ruin me. I can't stop staring as she comes apart under me and it causes me to push harder and faster, happy to overstay my welcome inside this place of paradise.

My cock throbs and my heart beats faster as I explode inside a woman who happened into my life by mistake. A chance encounter that has changed my life and as I empty my seed inside her, it's as if there is no end to it. The waves of ecstasy just keep on coming and I have never felt such sadness at having to pull out before. I want to stay, to know that she is mine and, more than anything, know she is safe.

CHAPTER 37

SERENA

*N*othing prepared me for that. My whole body is throbbing with delight, desire, and hope. That is the one emotion I am holding onto because Alexei has offered me something I never believed was mine to grasp with both hands. Can I leave with him? In my mind I already know the answer to that, but I want to try at least. To fight for something I want more than anything, and so as I hold him tightly, my head resting against his ripped chest, I vow to use every trick in the book to make it happen.

As we lie together on the couch, the fire warming our bodies with its wicked heat, I savor the moment when everything I want in life is holding me so fiercely in his arms.

He sits up and pulls me beside him, his fingers filtering through my hair as he whispers, "Say yes, Serena. Make it happen."

"I will do everything I can, Alexei, but we both know it's not really up to me."

He obviously doesn't like my answer and growls, "I will not walk away from this—from you. We have started something that is surprising but inevitable, and I won't let your family stand in the way of that."

"You may not be given a choice. Remember who you are dealing with." I say miserably and then, with a sigh, I gaze up at him and whisper, "I must go. Connor is waiting downstairs and I have already taken a chance being here at all."

He sighs heavily. "My car will arrive at your home at ten pm tomorrow night. You have until then to pack your bags and say your goodbyes and I will meet with your grandfather and assure him of your safety. One word from you and I will make it happen, Serena."

He shifts so his lips are against mine and he whispers, "I will give you the world, little one. Just say it's what you want, and I'll make it happen."

My heart is beating so fast it's the loudest sound in the room as I gaze into his glittering eyes and whisper, "I want it too, Alexei. I want you."

His lips crush against mine and his tongue forces its way inside, gripping mine in a show of passion that heats my blood. I can't walk away from him. I must try my best because I have never met a man like Alexei Romanov, and I already know I can't watch him leave.

As we kiss, I am desperate to cling to this moment. Almost as if it's the most important one in my life, but then my phone vibrates on the table where I left it, and reality comes crashing back to bite.

I tear myself away and say sorrowfully, "That will be Connor. Our time is up."

"Make him wait." Alexei growls and I shake my head sadly. "If I'm not home at the agreed time, my grandfather will send a small army to find me. They won't ask questions either. I will be dragged back and any argument I make to leave with you will not be looked upon kindly."

I touch his face gently and whisper, "Let me handle my family, Alexei. I am the only one who can. I must leave in order to stay."

He nods, the resignation in his eyes hard to witness and he says gruffly, "Okay. We have no choice, but tomorrow will be a day of goodbyes. It's up to you to determine who."

As I slip away from him and reach for my clothes, it's with a heavy heart. I want to leave with him so badly, but this will be a fight I'm not assured of winning.

Mafia is a way of life we are born into. As a woman in that world, I am to marry well to strengthen our power. To form an alliance between families, or to remain in my family and devote my life to it. Not travel the world as a rich man's plaything. I'm in no doubt that's what Alexei means. He has offered me nothing more than the trip of a lifetime. No assurances of happily ever after, just one wild, wicked adventure, that I'm almost positive my grandfather will turn down with a resounding 'go to hell.'

Alexei dresses and accompanies me downstairs to the underground car park where Connor is waiting. A strange mood has settled between us, and I hate it. It's almost as if we are both preparing ourselves for goodbye, and I detest every minute of it.

Connor is standing by the car with his usual menacing glower, and I sigh inside. Fuck my life and yet I really can't imagine it any other way.

As I settle inside the car, Alexei leans in and whispers, "Tomorrow night, Serena."

He slams the door behind him, and it may as well have had my heart in the way, because the pain inside me is almost too much to bear. That may be the last time I see Alexei Romanov and that is a very bitter pill to swallow.

CHAPTER 38

ALEXEI

I watch Serena leave with a heavy heart. There was something in her expression that told me I am losing her. She was resigned to her fate before she even tried to change it and that angers me. She should stand up and fight for what she wants, and I expect better of her. I know how her family works. Mine is the same, but my family allows a certain freedom that it appears hers does not.

As I head back up to my penthouse, I am angry, which surprises me. I don't get angry; I operate with zero emotion and cold calculation. Serena Vieri is the first woman who has tested every emotion I own and I'm not sure if I'm happy or appalled by it.

I head back into the penthouse and stare at the fire, the couch in disarray after our frantic coupling. As I lift one of the cushions, I hurl it across the room, knocking a lamp off the table holding it.

"Alexei." I turn to see Gleb watching me with a slight shake of his head and a glass of vodka in his hand that he offers to me.

"You will need this."

"Why?" I growl, taking it anyway and downing it in one second.

"We have a problem."

"Tell me." I'm almost grateful because problems are something I thrive on and excel at. Emotions, not so much.

"I ran a background check on the Vieri household as you asked."

I nod, wondering what he found. I instructed him to discover anything that could help me secure Serena by my side, so I could go to her grandfather with every weapon in my arsenal to get what I want.

"Serena's bodyguard, Connor."

My blood runs cold and I say quickly, "What about him?"

"That's not his real name."

"Tell me." It's as if ice is entering my blood and freezing me immobile as Gleb says in his usual expressionless voice.

"His real name is Marcello Lomas. He was a hit man for Carlos Matasso and operated under cover."

"Fuck!" I stare at him in disbelief as he continues.

"When Carlos died, the family had no don, and the soldiers found other employment. Apparently, Giselle Matasso arranged for Lomas to be appointed as Serena's bodyguard, vouching for him and his loyalty. When I checked his history, it was too contrived, alerting me to the fact it was probably re-written."

He shakes his head. "I sent his picture and some prints I lifted when he was offered our usual glass of refreshment for such purposes. It came back with an ID as Marcello Lomas and his resume almost corrupted my server."

"Why?"

Gleb shakes his head. "He is one of the finest hitmen in the country. His list of victims is long, and they are just the ones he is credited with. Usually, it means there are at least five times more bodies to add to the count of one. I dug a little deeper about this connection with Giselle and there was talk of a relationship between them several years ago. It appears they share a closer bond than most in their position, which is why I am concerned about Serena."

"Why?" The blood is heating in my veins as I sense I am not going to like what I hear and Gleb wastes no time in getting to the point.

"Giselle Matasso holds a deep burning hatred for her family. She arranged the death of her brother by spreading rumors in the right circles that he ordered a hit on his family. She broke up his marriage, and it appears hasn't finished yet."

"Serena." The pain hits me hard knowing I just sent her off with a man who may have been paid to kill her and Gleb nods, distaste flickering across his face.

"It appears that Giselle Matasso is hell bent on wiping out her family, and I believe Serena is in very imminent danger."

I waste no time and reach for my phone, shouting, "Prepare the car, grab the guards and make sure they are armed."

As I race to the elevator with Gleb close by my side, I call Serena in the hope she picks up.

There is nothing. It connects to voicemail, and I swear I age in seconds as I picture the worst.

As always, my men do not let me down and we head off in convoy, Gleb beside me, issuing my orders to the cars surrounding us.

"We must split up and cover every route to the Vieri mansion." I order.

"Gleb makes the call and I continue trying Serena's phone. In desperation, I make another call that I really don't want to make and as he answers, I hate the steel in his voice, knowing I am about to light a fuse that will only end in devastation.

"It's Serena."

The silence is almost palpable as I fill him in, knowing this is the best solution because they will have more reserves at their disposal. I'm taking a gamble with Serena's life, but something is telling me this is the right call. The only response I get when I relay the facts is an abrupt, *"Keep me informed."*

Then he cuts the call and I immediately try Serena again, praying she is safe and is only out of signal range. If I lose her now, it will break me apart, which tells me I'm a fool if I thought she was merely an itch to scratch. She is so much more than that and now I'm facing the possibility of losing her. If she survives, I am never letting her leave my side again.

CHAPTER 39

SERENA

I hated leaving Alexei, but circumstances are against us. Tonight was Killian's charity gala and tomorrow we celebrate my grandfather's birthday. He is in town for once and will be hosting a family dinner at his mansion. Everybody will be there except for one extremely important person to me. Alexei.

How I wish things were different, and I was a normal girl who could date at will without her family becoming involved. I already know that Alexei's proposition will receive a frosty reception.

Vieris don't run off unmarried and travel the world as a rich man's companion.

The women marry and are respected as the wife of a powerful man from a powerful family. Marriage was definitely not on offer and I'm doubting his request came with a lifetime condition attached. When the excitement wears off, I'll be returned to my family, probably broken hearted.

I should protect myself and walk away now, but I have never fallen so hard for any man before. I already know this goes further than infatuation and sex. It's him. The man behind the wicked smile and soulful eyes.

The power that surrounds him speaks to my soul. He is the man I would rather be waking up next to, than racing through the streets of Chicago back to my gilded cage.

I am so preoccupied with my thoughts, I don't register we have made a detour until I stare at unfamiliar scenery.

I tap on the screen and say loudly, "Connor, where are we heading?"

He completely ignores me, and my heart starts racing as I sense something is decidedly off about this.

I tap again. "Connor, where are we going?"

If anything, he increases the speed, and I am thrown back against the seat, my head hitting the corner of the window.

"Fuck!" I rub my head and a sense of danger creeps through my body, telling me something is very wrong with this situation.

I locate my purse and rummage for my phone, but it's not there. I search again and with a huff of frustration, I remember leaving it on Alexei's couch.

There is something very wrong about Connor's behavior and many reasons for that are suffocating me now. I am in danger; I already realize that. It's a premonition of something I may not survive and so I gather my wits around me like weapons.

I glare at him through the screen, noting how his eyes pierce right through me but hold no emotion.

I turn my face away and stare out at the passing scenery, formulating an escape plan in my mind. However, with no weapon to help me I conclude that I must sit and wait, knowing I have the element of surprise on my side.

* * *

It must be fifteen terrifying minutes later that he pulls into a parking lot, and I see a warehouse looming out of the shadows.

I will be safe until I get inside that building, which gives me some hope. I understand how these things work. My own family use places like this to interrogate victims and dispose of their bodies. It's obvious I'm being brought here for a reason, and I set my nerves back in place and wait for the opportune moment to escape.

The door slams and as he opens mine, he reaches inside and grabs my arm with a hoarse, "Don't fight me, Serena. It will only make it worse."

"Why are you doing this, Connor?"

I decide to act calm and try to reason with him because I'm not foolish enough to believe I stand a chance one on one with him.

"It's business, nothing more. Just do as I say."

I'm obviously not going to get any information from him, so I don't fight as he pulls me toward the warehouse and through a steel door.

The air is cold, and its icy fingers curl around my bare arms and whisper dark words of foreboding. The shadows offer no comfort from what could be lurking in them, and the stench of death hangs heavy in the air.

I am pulled toward the center of a massive room that was probably a hive of industry in the past. There are many businesses like this that collapsed when the dollar did and never recovered.

A lone chair sits in the gloom and I know what happens next and plead, "Please, Connor, don't do this. I will tell my grandfather you helped me. Whoever is paying you will never be a match for what we can offer you."

He says nothing at all and forces me into the chair and it's at this moment I realize I need to fight for my life and as I kick out, he removes his gun and holds it against my head.

"Game over, Serena." He growls as he holds a cloth over my nose and the strange scent is the last thing I remember as I drift into blissful unconsciousness.

* * *

A SHARP LIGHT wakes me and I blink as the light is directed in my eyes, momentarily blinding me.

"Wake up, honey." A woman's voice reaches me, and I blink as a figure swims into view.

I stare in disbelief at the familiar face as my Aunt Giselle stands regarding me with a slightly crazed expression in her eye.

"I'm so glad you made it to my party, Serena."

My aunt stands before me with a gun pointing at my head.

"What's going on?" I say fearfully, hating how weak my voice sounds.

"Revenge, honey. Pure, delicious revenge."

"For what?" I'm confused, and she laughs madly before snarling, "For my family's sins. The sins of my father, my mother, and my brother. You will follow your father to hell, and I will delight in watching the pain on my parent's faces as they lay you to rest, knowing there was nothing they could do to save you. They will understand how I felt when they killed my baby. They will live with the pain for the rest of their miserable lives knowing how that feels. To lose someone who meant everything and to know that I won in the end."

"What are you talking about?" I say it steadily because it's obvious my aunt is consumed by madness and she hisses, "They denied me a normal life. They told me my baby had died and forced me to marry a man who made my skin crawl. I despised him."

She snarls, her face etched with hatred, and snaps, "He never loved me. He used me to gain even more power. To become part of the Vieri family and find a way into the Dark Lords."

She shakes her head. "He was obsessed with it. Consumed by it and he tolerated me all the time my father was the Supreme Dark Lord."

She faces me and sneers, "I knew that as soon as my father

died, Carlos would dispose of me too. He hated being married to me. He brought his whores into our home and got one of the maids pregnant. He flouted his bastard son in my face, knowing I couldn't have children because of the complications my own child caused."

She stops and then cocks her head to one side. "Did you know I was raped, Serena?"

She sighs heavily. "By five men who thought it was a fun game. They weren't laughing when my father cut the smiles off their faces. I enjoyed that because I asked to be present. To watch them beg for mercy while his enforcer dismembered their bodies, starting with their dicks. They were castrated and then died a slow torturous death and yet it wasn't enough. I wanted more. Not marriage to a man who was no better than they were."

I watch her pace around the room, waving the gun in the air as she screeches. "Benito had it all. A loving wife who adored him, two sons and a daughter to make his family complete. He was a bastard, though. Much like Carlos was, and it didn't take much to convince him that we could have it all by cutting our father out."

She hisses. "He was weak, he always was. I was the strong one, but I was a woman. Women don't get to run mafia families. They must know their place and marry into them instead. I begged to succeed my father, but he laughed in my face. Then he arranged my marriage to Carlos and removed me from his protection."

"Why are you telling me this?" I interrupt and she turns, her eyes flashing in the darkened room.

"Because I want you to understand why you must die. I hate to do this, but I need to be cruel to be kind. You see, your fate will be no different from mine. You will not be heard and married off to someone of power who will strengthen the Vieri organization. I am sparing you from that, so you should thank me for my compassion because I wish someone had put a bullet through my brain rather than subject me to a lifetime with Carlos Matasso."

I watch as she grips the gun tighter and turns, a mad gleam in her eyes as she says sorrowfully, "I hate to be the one to do this, Serena, but you should blame your grandfather. Your brothers will also thank me when I arrange their own passing. I have already taken steps to bring their lives to an end. One by one, his soldiers will fall, and I will have won the game. My parents won't recover. There will be no one left to fight for them and the Dark Lords will move in and take over and I'll be free to live a happy retirement knowing justice has been done."

"You're mad." I say through gritted teeth, and she stops and stares at me with a crazed look in her eyes.

"I am your savior, Serena. You should thank me."

She turns and appears to wipe a tear from her eye, and I'm suddenly aware of Connor behind me. He cuts the ties binding me and presses his gun in my hand and my heart beats so fast I can hardly catch my breath. He is helping me. I don't understand why, but I will not waste this golden opportunity.

I take a deep breath as my aunt turns and raises the gun to my head and I whisper, "Please, Aunt Giselle. Don't shoot me in cold blood. I don't want to die alone. Please will you hold me."

She leans down and stares into my eyes with tears pouring down her face and she strokes my cheek with the gun and whispers, "You are so beautiful, Serena. I always thought of you as the daughter I lost. She would have been around your age, and I watched you grow with a heart full of sadness at what I was denied."

She strokes my face and then leans down and kisses me softly on the lips and her gun is just behind my head. The tears are wet against my lashes as I struggle to keep my emotions in check and she whispers, "Please forgive me, my child. I love you, but this is how it must be."

I sense her hand moving behind me and, wasting no time at all, in a quick movement, I grip the gun and before she can react, I force it between us and pull the trigger. Her own gun falls to the ground as a shot rings out. She staggers back as I push her and note the open wound leaking blood from her chest.

As she falls to the ground, she stares up at me in shock and I stand above her body and feel my eyes flashing as I say darkly, "That's for my father, you wicked bitch. Say hi to him in hell."

I empty the gun right between her eyes and stare as the life drains from her body, a horrified expression of defeat on her face.

The gun smokes in my hand as I stare at her life seeping away along with her blood on the concrete, and then we hear loud voices and a commotion outside. I look up as the room fills with soldiers armed with machine guns and don't fuck with me attitudes. As my brothers push through, I drop the gun and say darkly, "It's good of you to show up."

Killian stares at our aunt's body and growls, "Fuck."

Shade merely laughs out loud.

"Way to go, sis. That bitch had it coming."

Killian nods to Connor and says in his husky voice, "Thank you."

I stare between them and say in confusion. "What's going on?"

"I'll tell you back at the house."

"No!" I yell. "You will tell me now, Killian, because I fucking deserve the truth."

Killian nods to the guards and says calmly, "Leave us."

He stares at Connor. "Except you."

As the guards leave, it's just the four of us along with Aunt Giselle's dead body and a rage boiling inside me that means I am liable to do something I may regret.

CHAPTER 40

ALEXEI

*W*e drive around in circles and the frustration is killing me. Gleb is constantly on his phone as he pulls up information to help us.

We get a call that Connor's car was heading east of the city and Gleb runs a search on the area. He narrows it down to three possible locations and we scatter our guards to search every individual one. We head to a part of town that is full of trouble. Poverty, desperate drug users and individuals who take their chances because they have nothing left to lose.

As we crawl along the streets, we attract unwanted attention that is soon scattered when our machine guns make an appearance. I am out of control and liable to shoot anyone that messes with me and as my guards do their job and question likely informants at gunpoint, the only intel we get is that we are more likely to find what we're looking for at a disused warehouse on the southeast point of town.

My guard 'persuades' the informant to join him in return for a handful of dollars and his life spared and we head off following his directions.

I can tell we have the right place when I see the cars filling the area and I pray to God Killian got here first.

As we vacate the cars, his guards form a wall of menace between us and I step forward and say roughly, "Let us through."

They shake their heads and I yell, "Fucking let me through if you don't want to start a god-damned war."

My own men are armed and equally as dangerous and the guard says respectfully, "Wait one minute."

He says something in his earpiece and then points to me. "Only you." My bodyguard makes to protest, and I snarl, "Leave it, Viktor. I go in alone."

I hand my gun to him, demonstrating I am not armed, knowing if Serena's brothers are there no harm will come to her, if she's still alive that is.

My heart is heavy as I head inside the huge space, hoping like crazy they were in time. As I enter, I'm so relieved when I see Serena standing over a dead body, glaring at her brothers with fury blazing from her eyes. She looks like a warrior. A beautiful, amazing fucking goddess and then she turns that imperious gaze to me and her expression changes as the mask slips.

She wastes no time and runs into my arms and sobs on my shoulder, and as my arms fold around her, I stare at her brothers with cold fury.

"What happened?"

Killian sighs. "Our aunt happened."

Serena pulls away from me and says one word that changes my life.

"Yes."

I stare at her beautiful face in shock and whisper, "You mean…"

I don't finish my sentence as she whispers, "I'll go with you."

Shade says lazily, "I'm sorry to interrupt this happy moment, but we have shit to deal with here."

My arm remains around Serena's shoulders as she faces her brothers and says angrily, "You have a lot of explaining to do."

Killian nods. "You deserve to know the truth."

He casts a disparaging glare at his aunt's body and snarls. "Connor's real name is Marcello Lomas. He was a hit man for the Matassos."

Connor says nothing as Serena stares at him in shock.

Killian continues. "He came to us with information, and we acted accordingly."

"Information? I don't understand."

Serena is trembling and I tighten my hold around her.

"He was ordered to hit Serena by our aunt, and she would pay him enough money to retire if he included all three of us."

Killian's eyes glitter as he hisses, "She wanted to bring the family down. Marcello told me she had spread word that our father ordered a hit on us, knowing we would get to him first."

My heart goes out to him because it was Killian who arranged his own father's death on the instruction of his grandfather.

Serena gasps beside me and Killian snarls, "Marcello's loyalty has always been to the Dark Lords, but he went along with her plan under my instruction."

Serena shakes her head. "You knew he was going to kill me."

Shade laughs out loud. "Like fuck he was. Marcello was *protecting* you. He was your protection when you left for Australia but was acting as a double agent. How was he to know you would give him the slip and plan your own journey? He was there to keep you safe and then you weren't– there I mean." He shakes his head and stares at me with a hint of impatience.

"You always were stubborn, Serena, but even we didn't see this one coming." He jerks his thumb at me and says softly, "As it turned out, you were in safe hands."

Killian adds. "Marcello agreed to see this through to the end because we needed Aunt Giselle to play her hand."

"So, you used me as a fucking target? You bastards!" Serena

yells and I have to hold her back in case she uses the gun on the other members of her family.

"You were never in danger, Serena." Killian says darkly. "Marcello is trained and was always on your side. There were also marksmen in the shadows with their guns trained on our aunt. There was also the added precaution of no bullets in her gun. She was never going to kill anyone."

"You set her up." Serena's eyes are wide as Killian nods.

"We needed the truth. There was too much riding on this. One dead family member is enough. We didn't want any mistakes this time."

"Does nonno know?" Serena's voice shakes as she stares at the corpse at her feet, and Killian nods. "He ordered us to dispose of her. It broke his heart."

It's as if all the fight has left her as she sags against me, brushing the tears away furiously with her fingers as she realizes what just happened.

She breaks away and runs toward her brothers, who crowd around her, and as they shut the rest of us out, they share a moment only a family can. A family who has lived, breathed and dealt with who they are and what they must do because of it. A family in grief and facing the pain of betrayal, a far more devastating cross to bear than threats from strangers.

We wait in silence for them to come to terms with what happened here today and their part in it. Then, as they pull away, I notice the cool mask of zero emotion has been set back in place.

Serena gazes at me with a smile that lights up her eyes and holds out her hand.

"Take me home, Alexei. We're done here."

Her brothers look on as she says over her shoulder. "I'll see you tomorrow and tell nonna I'll be bringing a plus one."

As we leave, she doesn't look back and the guards part as we step outside and watch silently as we head to my car. As we step inside, she says nothing at all and laces my fingers with hers and says in a stronger voice. "It appears that our adventure will continue, Alexei, whether my family agrees or not."

She turns and smiles and I believe this is the moment when I fall deeply in love with Serena Vieri. There is no going back now for either of us. What began as an impetuous invitation has ended as being the most important decision of my life.

CHAPTER 41

SERENA

THE NEXT DAY

J am not worried, nervous, or fearful. I killed my aunt in cold blood last night and I would do it again in a heartbeat.

What happened was do or die and I am at peace with that. If anything, I did her a favor because her fate had already been sealed.

Alexei held me until I fell asleep in his arms. He was there for me when I needed him most, and I will never forget that. He faced my family with no fear, and I admire that about him. He came for me knowing I was in danger and that means everything to me.

Now we are heading to my grandparents' mansion for the birthday dinner that will go ahead as planned, with one person missing at the table.

We will mourn our aunt's passing as is customary, but nobody will be sad to see her go. She has torn this family apart, and it was a necessary conclusion and the only people who concern me now are my grandparents, who must live with the knowledge that both of their children plotted against them.

At least they have us. Their grandchildren and we will come together as a family before I set off on my travels, whether they agree or not.

We make our way up the driveway after clearing security and I grip Alexei's hand hard.

"Are you ready for this?"

He nods with a twinkle in his eye. "I almost feel sorry for them, little tiger."

"Don't be. They can handle whatever shit is flung their way. They are Vieris and have fought their entire lives. This is an easy battle to concede."

I lean forward and kiss him softly, loving how peaceful he makes me. It's as if I'm not on my own anymore and it's good knowing there is a strong man beside me who is my equal in every way. He doesn't try to dominate me, to belittle me or to control me. He accepts me for who I am and inevitably I am falling hard and fast for my fearless Russian.

As soon as we reach the front door, the car stops outside and one of my grandfather's guards opens it and peers inside.

"Miss Vieri, Mr. Romanov. Welcome."

He steps aside and we head toward the open door, and I am extremely nervous after what happened last night.

I killed their daughter.

I'm guessing my welcome won't be the usual one and yet as soon as I step inside the familiar hallway, nonna is waiting with a concerned expression on her face.

"Serena." Her eyes fill with tears as she pulls me into her usual warm embrace, and I can't help but sob in her arms as the relief hits me hard.

"I'm so sorry, Nonna." I weep for her loss, and she whispers,

"You have nothing to be sorry about. You did it to protect this family and we will always back you on that."

"You're not mad at me." I pull back and stare at her anxiously and she wipes a tear from her eye and whispers, "I could never be prouder of you than I am now. You are a true Vieri, Serena. You did what was right in the moment. You were faced with losing your life, so how could I be angry about the decision you made?"

She says sorrowfully, "Giselle was an extremely disturbed woman. I should have addressed this years ago. I blame myself."

I stare at her with a fierce expression. "You did *everything* for her. She is solely to blame for this."

Nonna smiles and then stares past me at Alexei, who is watching the scene with interest, and she grins.

"Mr. Romanov. I believe you have been corrupting my grand-daughter." She says it with a twinkle in her eye and he nods respectfully.

"I am guilty as charged, Mrs. Vieri, but I can assure you I only have her best interests at heart."

"I appreciate your honesty…"

"Alexei. Please."

"Alexei."

She smiles warmly. "Before we join the others, Don Vieri would like to see you both in his office."

My heart sinks as nonna whispers. "Don't worry, Serena. You can do no wrong in your grandfather's eyes. You never could."

She kisses me on both cheeks and says firmly, "Now don't keep him waiting any longer. Dinner will soon be served, and nothing must interfere with that."

I nod and turn to Alexei and reach for his hand.

"We may as well get this over with. Nonna's right. Even business comes second to one of her meals."

* * *

As we head in the familiar direction, I am strangely nervous. It's unusual to be summoned to my grandfather's office without my brothers for support. I'm guessing I have a lot of explaining to do and so I whisper, "Perhaps it's best if I handle this. We must get on his right side if we want him to agree to our plans."

Alexei smiles and I detect the humor in his eyes. "Of course. You know best, little one."

He winks, and it makes me smile because having him beside me makes everything better.

We head to my grandfather's den, and I knock on the door before pushing it open. As we step inside, I take a deep breath because I've always loved the smell inside his personal space. Cigar smoke laced with brandy fumes. A real man's den and in my eyes, there is no better real man than my grandfather.

He is sitting behind his desk with the ever-present unlit cigar held between his fingers. As he glances up, I note the pain in his eyes and feel completely responsible for that.

"I'm sorry." I say with a sob, and he shakes his head and crooks his finger, summoning me to his side.

I can't get there fast enough, and he stands and takes me into his arms and pulls me close, sighing heavily. "If anything happened to you, princess, there would have been hell to pay."

I cry on his shoulder as he whispers, "You mean everything to me, and I can confirm you were never in any danger. I made certain of that."

"You should have told me." I say with anger, and he growls, "It had to be that way. Giselle was always a loose cannon, and I blame myself for not dealing with her sooner. However, I reiterate, you were *never* in any danger. Connor was there for you, not her."

"I wish I'd known that at the time." I'm still pissed they used me in this way and then something strikes me that I hadn't considered until now.

I pull back and stare at him with a hard expression that irritatingly only appears to please him.

"You knew about this all along and you never once thought to tell me. Killian and Shade knew, but you sent me off to Australia in ignorance. How long have you known?"

I glare at him, and he shrugs. "Long enough."

"Connor placed the gun in my hand." I think out loud and then face him with a furious hiss.

"You set me up to kill her for you. Killian and Shade said there were marksmen with trained rifles on her and you still set me up. Why?"

My grandfather points to the chairs set in front of his desk and says in his low drawl.

"Sit and I will explain."

He nods to Alexei and says coolly, "Mr. Romanov. There is much to discuss, but first I will address Serena's question."

He taps the cigar on his desk and stares at us with his penetrating glare that defies anyone to interrupt.

"Serena."

He fixes me with a hard expression. "For your entire life, you have asked to become part of this business, equal to your brothers."

I open my mouth but close it quickly, knowing better than to interrupt him.

"You have been extremely vocal on the subject, insisting you are more than capable of the job, whatever it involves."

"So, this was a test of that?" I can't help blurting out and he smiles softly, "If you like. You see, I can deny you nothing at all. You already know that but taking another person's life is something you never get used to. You acted in self defense, and you had no choice, or so you thought. So, in answer to your question, yes, it was a test and now I have my answer."

He smiles with approval. "You are worthy to take your place in the family business, if that is the path you wish to travel."

I can't believe it. The bastard actually set me up to murder my aunt. Who the fuck does that?

I lean back in my seat and stare at him in horror, realizing that to work in the family business, you must leave your humanity at the door. I already know my brothers think nothing of taking a life. I truly believe Shade enjoys it. But me. Am I really cut out for this shit just to prove I'm their equal? I'm not so sure anymore.

My grandfather turns to Alexei and considers him carefully. Then he says respectfully, "My condolences on the death of your father. I knew him well, and he was a good man and a valuable business associate."

Alexei replies, "Thank you. He always spoke highly of you too, sir."

I watch his eyes narrow and the chill in the air increases as he says slowly, "But there is the matter of my granddaughter to address. I believe you offered her a ride to Australia. What was your intention?"

I am cringing with mortification and open my mouth to defend him, but Alexei silences me by saying quickly. "I was intrigued by Serena from the moment I first set eyes on her. I realized her guard was inadequate, which irritated me."

"Inadequate?" My grandfather raises his eyes and Alexei nods.

"It was easy to detain him and move in and steal her from him. That would never happen in my organization, Don Vieri. I can assure you of that."

"I see." He scrawls something on his notepad and says gruffly, "Continue."

Alexei's voice doesn't falter as he says firmly, "Serena intrigued me and when I discovered who she really was, I arranged the call between you. At no time was she in danger and I only had her best interests at heart."

"Is that so?" My grandfather actually laughs out loud.

"Mr. Romanov. I have not always been an old man. I understand how these things work, and I'm aware of the interest you had in my granddaughter. If she wasn't so enamored of you, I would be conducting this meeting in a different place entirely."

"Stop!" I shake my head in horror. "Please, nonno. Alexei never knew who I was and when he discovered it, he did everything possible to keep me safe, unlike my own family, I might add, which leads me to tell you the reason I brought him here."

"Go on." He leans back in his chair and appears almost amused as I say bravely, "Alexei has asked me to travel with him indefinitely and I've said yes."

"I see." My grandfather looks between the two of us and then sighs heavily.

"Under what terms, Mr. Romanov?"

"As my equal, Don Vieri. As my companion and well, the woman I want to get to know on a deeper level."

"So, not marriage then."

I blush furiously as my grandfather sighs. "It is something I don't understand, but I accept the world is changing."

He transfers his attention to me and smiles. "Serena. You are a modern woman, and the old ways no longer interest you. I understand your need to travel and see the world, enjoying a freedom of sorts. I am not unaware of such things, and I envy you the freedom of choice you have. I give you my blessing on the condition that you return home to visit once every eight weeks. At the end of the year, I expect to see some form of commitment between you."

He turns to Alexei and says roughly, "My granddaughter deserves your respect. Alexei and I expect you to treat her with honor and care. She is not someone to fool around with and then discard in favor of another. She is your equal and you will not forget that."

Alexei turns to me and reaches for my hand.

"I know the power of your granddaughter, sir, and if anyone should be worried, it's me."

His reply makes my grandfather laugh out loud, and he sets his cigar down and nods toward the door.

"Then our business is concluded. Your request is approved, Serena, and should you decide to return home and take up a position in the family business, the door is always open."

"Thank you." Tears almost blind me as I head to my grandfather's side and hug him tightly, burying my face in his neck and whispering, "I love you so much. Thank you."

For a second, he holds me close and says nothing, but I feel the emotion between us as a tangible force. He is the head of the Vieri mafia. The supreme ruler of the Dark Lords and the most feared head of a well-respected family, but he will always be my grandfather to me.

We head out to meet the rest of the family, with two places vacant but set all the same. Two traitors who don't deserve the recognition they are getting who turned against their family and suffered the consequences of that.

As we take our seats, I am warm inside as we celebrate my grandfather's birthday like any other family in the country. My brothers have found love and appear happy, and so have I.

I turn to Alexei and reach for his hand under the table, loving that our adventure will continue. The threats have gone for now because every single person at this table knows the value of family, even a fucked-up one like this.

CHAPTER 42

DON VIERI

*B*irthdays. How I hate them. The beginning of life and a milestone to be tolerated every single year.

I have experienced many of them in varying circumstances. This one will be remembered for a very important reason.

Serena has left already with Alexei Romanov, and I couldn't be happier for her. He is an honorable, powerful man and will keep her safe. If I know anything, it's the Romanovs are the most feared family in Russia and deal with their shit in a far more brutal way than we even do. I will never understand the way they operate, but I know Alexei will have a challenge with Serena. She is nobody's fool and will keep him guessing. At least she is one less person for me to worry about.

My two grandsons sit before me, a glass of bourbon in their hands as their wife and girlfriend chat shit with Ariana and I sigh as I return to the business in hand.

I raise my glass and say huskily, "Today we mourn the passing of my daughter and your aunt Giselle. God rest her soul."

They lift their glasses, and we drain them in one, slamming them down on the table and then face one another with serious expressions.

I stare at Killian and say firmly, "Are you good?"

"I am," he replies, and I repeat the question to Shade, who nods. "Of course."

If anything, it saddens me that there is no emotion in their hearts for their aunt's passing. Her threat to murder their sister dealt with that. Their family loyalty is unquestionable and yet I have a huge gaping hole in my heart now both my children have gone. They betrayed me and sought to destroy both me and Ariana and I will never recover from that.

"We have a problem." I get straight down to business and, as always, it captures their attention.

They lean forward with excitement, and it makes me smile inside. I trust my grandsons with my life and know they will never let me down. At least I did something right.

I lean forward and say gruffly, "Giselle had a child. A girl."

They say nothing and I think back on a painful time in my life.

"She was the result of a savage act of rape. The men involved were dealt with, and Giselle saw out the term of her pregnancy on our island, Serenita."

I still deal with the raw pain I experienced when Giselle gave birth and I say sadly, "It was a difficult birth. Your aunt was in a lot of pain and no meds appeared to help. She was angry, determined she would hate the baby and begged us to dispose of her."

They say nothing but stare back at me with hardened expressions and I shake my head.

"The baby was born and struggled to breathe. It was only the quick reaction of the doctor that saved her life."

"Saved her?" Shade leans forward. "I thought Aunt Giselle said she died. What happened?"

"That's what we told her." I say gravely, registering the shock on their faces.

"She survived, but your aunt was in no place mentally to care for her, and I was afraid for the small child. We have all seen the woman my daughter became, and we took steps to protect the child."

Killian exhales sharply. "So, she's still alive?"

"Yes. She is."

I think back on the decision we made at the time and still experience the pain of regret at what we did.

"She was adopted by a good family. She has two parents who are god-fearing and raised her well."

I sigh heavily. "She is close to Serena in age and knows nothing at all about her hard beginning. I set up a trust fund for her that pays all her expenses and keeps her in the manner I expect as a Vieri."

"So, what's the problem?" Killian asks and I growl.

"Her identity has been compromised, and she has been offered a job by one of my enemies. A man who wants to remove us from the Dark Lords and will use her to discredit us. He is aware of her past and the lengths I went to deal with the men responsible for her birth. This whole affair could be exposed, and we must stop that from happening."

"How?" Shade asks, the gleam in his eye telling me he is already relishing the challenge and I say gruffly, "We discover his secrets and use them against him."

"What is his name?" Killian says darkly, and I love the fire in his eyes as he rises to the challenge.

"Troy Remington."

"The CEO of Remington industries?"

"Yes." I sigh and stare at my two grandsons, who have all the eagerness of youth, and say firmly. "Your cousin's name is Laura Kincaid."

I picture the woman who is blissfully unaware of her heritage and hope she never discovers her painful beginnings.

"You must protect her at all costs, which means she must *not* find out who her parents were. She is a good, decent kid who has done well. She knows nothing of our world, and I want it to stay that way. Remove the threat from her life and leave her in blissful ignorance. I am counting on you to eliminate the next threat in our quest quickly and under the radar. That is all I ask."

I open my desk drawer and pull out two identical folders, sliding one each of their way and I say in a hardened tone, "We will face many threats from The Dark Lords, but they will never seize control of our organization. Troy Remington just made a big mistake. Make certain he regrets it."

As they seize the folders, I watch the spark in their eyes ignite and know this is in safe hands. I almost pity Troy Remington because when a Vieri has you in his sights, there will be no escaping your fate.

EPILOGUE

LAURA

*T*he town is busy, busier than normal, and I'm resorted to pushing my way through the sea of bodies in the Brew House. The aroma of coffee and warm pastries hits me, and I take a deep breath to savor the moment. I much prefer places like this to bars and clubs. There's a coziness here that speaks to my soul.

I've never been into late nights out, resulting in drunken stupors. I prefer warm, cozy evenings in front of a movie with a warm cookie and a mug of coffee by my side. My friends say I'm boring. They are probably right.

It was the same at school. I was the geek. The student most likely to succeed or the one expected to wind up married at twenty-one, living a suburban life. Both suit me just fine because I like everything orderly and its place, the way life is supposed to be.

"Laura, over here."

Gemma waves at me from across the crowded coffee shop. She is tucked in a booth near the back, one of only a few who are shielded from view, and I head over with a broad smile on my face because I have news.

"Where's Brittany?" I say, glancing around as if she will materialize out of thin air from Potter's invisibility cloak.

"She messaged to say she's on her way. Late as usual."

Gemma rolls her eyes and points to the latte she has already purchased on my behalf.

"It should still be hot enough. It's crazy in here today, so I thought I'd get the orders in advance."

"Good thinking." I settle in the booth and stretch out my feet, loving how warm and cozy it is in the cool January air. It's a new year that brings hope and new beginnings and I am a walking advertisement for that.

"Sorry guys, the subway was a bitch today."

"When isn't it?" Gemma shakes her head as Brittany slides in beside her, seizing the double shot cappuccino that she appears addicted to.

"Thanks honey, I'll ping you the money."

"No need, you can get the next ones."

They gaze at me expectantly as I shift on my seat and Brittany grins.

"Okay, Laura, what's the big news? Please say you've got yourself a man at last, but not Oscar Calahan. That dude is bad news."

I hate that my heart leaps at the mention of the guy my heart can't unattach itself from. My high school crush who decided to give me a chance one night at a frat party. I was in love, he was in lust, and it didn't end well for me.

"It's not him." I shake my head, hating the pity on their faces.

"No, it's way more exciting than that."

"You got laid at last," Gemma says hopefully and this time I roll my eyes.

"I wish you would get over this obsession with my sex life. I'm happy being single and preparing for my future as a cat lady."

"Then tell us already, because I'm bursting over here."

Brittany leans forward, her eyes alight with interest.

I take a deep breath and say with pride. "I've got a job."

They stare at me in amazement.

"A job?" Gemma sounds slightly disappointed about that.

"Is that it? A freaking job. I've got two, and it's hardly breaking news."

"Yes, but it's not just a job, it's *the* job."

"I don't understand. A job's a job."

Brittany stares moodily into her coffee. "Why is that exciting?"

I play my trump card.

"Because it's as the personal assistant of Troy Remington."

Now I have their attention.

Gemma whistles and Brittany claps her hands with excitement.

"Wow! That is news." Her eyes shine. "Troy Remington, huh? The most eligible bachelor in Chicago, Troy Remington. The heir to billions and so drop dead gorgeous he could model underwear on the runway at Paris fashion week, Troy Remington."

"The Troy Remington who could burn a woman's panties off with one lustful glare from his turbulent dirty eyes Troy Remington?" Gemma says wistfully, and it makes me giggle.

"Yes. I told you I had news."

"This is life changing, Laura."

Gemma's eyes are so wide it's strangely comical and Brittany sighs dreamily. "Imagine your one on ones with him. Make sure you wear a short skirt and no panties. Cross your legs several times and flutter your eyelashes."

"Yes and lean over his desk and ask if he likes his coffee hot, as you flash him your cleavage." Gemma giggles and it makes me laugh out loud.

"He's probably got a girlfriend. Guys like that always do."

"Or a boyfriend." Brittany giggles and Gemma says with a sigh. "No. That man fucks women before breakfast, lunch, and dinner. I've stalked him online so much I'm surprised I haven't had a visit from the cops with a restraining internet order."

"Me too." I giggle. "When my agency called and told me I was in line for the job, I stalked the hell out of him and I don't mind telling you, I had a few hot nights imagining what it would be like."

"What do you mean and please say hot sex over his desk?" Brittany giggles and I nod.

"Of course. That man is so hot he could boil this coffee with one look alone."

"Does he have a girlfriend?" Gemma says with curiosity, and I groan.

"Several if you believe the internet. I clicked on 'images' and there were dozens of glamorous women on his arm."

Brittany sighs. "Lucky bitches. I bet he's a bastard in the sack. All dominant and brooding. What I wouldn't give for a night with him."

"And now you get to spend every day with him, you lucky bitch." Brittany says jealously and Gemma adds.

"I'm guessing he travels a lot. You will be required to accompany him."

"Wow, get him drunk one night and you may be in with a chance." Brittany laughs and I say in mock anger, "Hey, I'm not that bad."

"True, you can hold your own in a room of freaking nerds but look at what you're wearing."

I glance down at my sweater dress that covers my neck and every curve of my body. My UGG boots are warm and cozy but show nothing of my legs and the thick hat and scarf I added for good measure cover the rest of me perfectly against the chill of winter outside.

"You've got to up your game, my lucky friend."

Gemma says thoughtfully. "There's a personal shopper in Bloomingdales my cousin can recommend. It's a bit pricey though. Did they mention the salary?"

"Only more than I made all year in the pet store. I'm living the dream, ladies."

I grin as they stare at me with pure envy and Gemma sighs. "I bet he fucks like a pro."

"Yes. All positions considered and anything goes." Brittany adds with a dreamy expression on her face.

"I bet he's a dirty bastard." I giggle. "He has that look about him. Polished and respectable in public, but an animal between the sheets."

"Against the wall." Gemma giggles.

"Over the desk." Brittany grins.

"In the back seat of the car." I smile softly.

"In a dark alley." Brittany imagines out loud and then we stop because someone stands beside our table and as we look up, the blood drains from our faces as we stare into the glittering eyes of the man himself. Troy Remington.

He gazes at each one of us in turn and in my mortified trance, I can only register how immaculate he looks. He is wearing black jeans that hug his hips and a cream sweater under a black suede jacket. A Burberry scarf is wound around his neck and his brown leather belt looks new and expensive.

He stares at us with cool derision and says in a firm voice.

"For your information. Yes, I do fuck like a pro, and my preferred position is on top. Some may call me an animal between the sheets, but I prefer to dominate my women on top of them. I have been known to enjoy sex outdoors, but down a dark alley is seriously low on my preferred list of places. On a yacht, a private plane and on a beach in paradise are more my style."

He stares at our horrified faces and smirks. "I have no current girlfriend, but I enjoy a crowded little black book and there is no shortage of women to call on should I feel the need to bend one over my desk and fuck them from behind. Contrary to your beliefs, I can't boil coffee with one look, which is why my assistants do it for me."

He stares at me with a hard expression, and I try desperately to disappear into my seat as he says firmly, "I travel a lot but don't expect my companions to perform anything other than their contracted duties and, more than anything, I value their discretion."

I cringe as he drops a business card on the table and snaps, "Report to Celeste Weaver at Saks on Monday morning at eight am. You will be fitted for suitable business attire because I have standards and my assistant must meet them all. They include not gossiping about me in crowded public places and to sign a non-disclosure agreement before they start."

He glares at us all each in turn and I swear we age right before his eyes as a woman moves by his side and stares at us with a slight shake of her head, the pitying glance she throws our way concealing the slight hint of amusement attempting to break through.

"Shall we?" Troy nods to the woman who appears to have stepped from the cover of Vogue and as they head off, we watch them leave along with our power of speech.

TROY

Melissa chuckles beside me as we step out of the coffee shop and says in a low voice, "That went better than expected."

"It did." I smile as I consider how mortified my new assistant must be feeling now.

Melissa grins. "It was probably more than you bargained for when you decided to listen in for information."

"It was enough."

We step into the chauffeur driven limo and Melissa shivers.

"Those places remind me of when I was made to work a weekend job through college. Never take me there again."

"It was a necessary evil." I shrug, pulling out my phone and noting the twenty-five texts and several voicemail messages waiting.

"What are your plans now?" She says, gazing out of the window at the busy streets outside.

"Work, of course."

"Of course."

She shakes her head. "You really should try to have some fun occasionally, Troy. All work and no play make Troy exceedingly dull."

"I play, Melissa. After I work."

"A quick dinner followed by a fuck isn't really what I had in mind. Really Troy, you're missing out on living."

"I'm breathing, aren't I?"

She sighs with exasperation.

"I'll never understand the men in this family."

"You don't need to understand us, sis. Just enjoy the lifestyle we provide."

"You really are an ass, Troy. Talking of which, I said I'd meet Harrison later. He wants my opinion on a new house in Burr Ridge."

"What is he, an old man now?" I sigh with irritation because Harrison Remington is even more of a player than I am.

"Who knows what runs through his head? I'm just the plus one in all your lives when you want a cover story."

I lean back and think of the reason we went to the Brew House at all. I've had Laura Kincaid followed for months now. It was an interesting meeting with my private investigator, who discovered who she really is. He found out she was fresh out of university and seeking employment in the business sector with Hariges employment agency. It didn't take much to fire my current assistant, who was worse than useless anyway, and arrange Laura Kincaid's employment instead.

Yes. She will soon learn that I get what I want and right now I want her for a very important reason. To gain control of the empire her grandfather formed and remove her criminal family from the secret society he founded. The Dark Lords have become bigger than the Vieris and there is no room in it for anything other than reputable businessmen and men of power. She doesn't know she has mafia blood running through her veins because she was adopted at birth. Until now, she was living a respectable life with good honest people who have kept her secret well.

She doesn't know it yet, but Laura Kincaid is my key to the throne room and her grandfather will have no choice but to agree to my terms if he wants to keep his dirty little secret hidden, or face his past blowing up and devastating his perfect world.

If you want to read what happens next, check out Born Evil

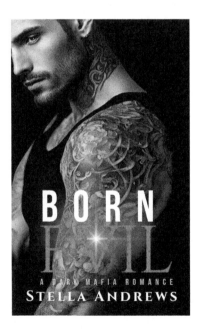

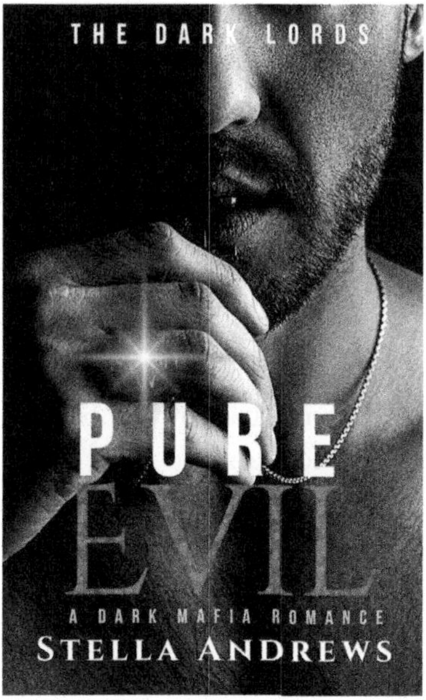

Pure Evil
Killian & Purity's story

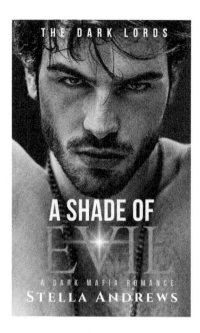

A Shade of Evil

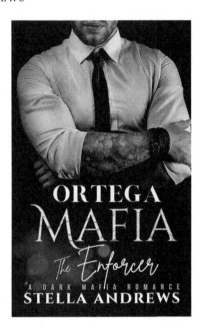

If you want to read about The Ortega's and Carlos & Giselle
Matasso, check out
Ortega Mafia.

Thank you for reading this story.
If you have enjoyed the fantasy world of this novel, please would
you be so kind as to leave a review?

Join my closed Facebook Group

Stella's Sexy Readers

Follow me on Instagram

Carry on reading for more Reaper Romances, Mafia Romance & more.
Remember to grab your free book by visiting stellaandrews.com.

ALSO BY STELLA ANDREWS

Twisted Reapers

Rebel
Dirty Hero (Snake & Bonnie)
Daddy's Girls (Ryder & Ashton)
Twisted (Sam & Kitty)
The Billion Dollar baby (Tyler & Sydney)
Bodyguard (Jet & Lucy)
Flash (Flash & Jennifer)
Country Girl (Tyson & Sunny)
Brutal Sinner (Jonny & Faith)

The Romanos
The Throne of Pain (Lucian & Riley)
The Throne of Hate (Dante & Isabella)
The Throne of Fear (Romeo & Ivy)
Lorenzo's story is in Broken Beauty

Beauty Series
*Breaking Beauty (Sebastian & Angel) ***
Owning Beauty (Tobias & Anastasia)
*Broken Beauty (Maverick & Sophia) ***
Completing Beauty – The series

Five Kings
Catch a King (Sawyer & Millie) *

<u>Slade</u>

Steal a King

Break a King

Destroy a King

Marry a King

Baron

Club Mafia

Club Mafia – The Contract

Club Mafia – The Boss

Club Mafia – The Angel

Club Mafia – The Savage

Club Mafia - The Beast

Club Mafia – The Demon

Ortega Mafia

The Enforcer

The Consigliere

The Don

The Dark lords

Pure Evil

A Shade of Evil

Pretty Evil

Standalone

The Highest Bidder (Logan & Samantha)

Rocked (Jax & Emily)

Brutally British

Deck the Boss

Printed in Great Britain
by Amazon

39043384R00142